SO
over it

Books by Stephanie Morrill

THE REINVENTION OF SKYLAR HOYT

Me, Just Different
Out with the In Crowd
So Over It

The Reinvention of Skylar Hoyt, book 3

so
over it

the reinvention of skylar hoyt

STEPHANIE MORRILL

Revell

a division of Baker Publishing Group
Grand Rapids, Michigan

Published by Revell
a division of Baker Publishing Group
P.O. Box 6287, Grand Rapids, MI 49516-6287
www.revellbooks.com

Printed in the United States of America

Library of Congress Cataloging-in-Publication Data is on file at the Library of Congress, Washington DC.

10   11   12   13   14   15   16   7   6   5   4   3   2   1

For my daughter, McKenna Noelle.
Thanks for being your sunny, silly, creative self.
Love you, girl.

1

My eyes, innocently grazing the new releases at Block-buster, locked on Connor Ross.

I would've avoided him, especially since he stood there with Jodi, but we held eye contact too long to pretend we hadn't noticed each other.

We exchanged awkward smiles—what else could we do?—and moved closer.

"Hey," I said, being my usual creative self.

"Hi." His smile hung crooked. It didn't always. Just when he felt uncomfortable. Connor hadn't flashed me a straight smile since March. Three months and six days ago.

"Hi, Skylar." Jodi infused her voice with warmth.

I managed to raise the corners of my mouth. I couldn't trust myself to speak actual words to her. Even when I said simple things like, "Hi," it always sounded angry and bitter. Two things I felt, but had no intention of her knowing.

"What are you guys doing here?" I asked, then nearly cringed. Hello—what else would they be doing at Block-buster?

Connor acted nice about it. "Trying to find a movie that'll make everyone happy."

"Not an easy task."

"Cevin's the real toughie," Connor said with a grin.

Both Jodi and I laughed—Cevin's the Ross family's dog—then stopped and looked at each other. So awkward.

"Well. I better go." I waved the case of my selected movie, as if to prove my hasty departure had nothing to do with them, that I was, in fact, ready to leave. "Abbie's waiting in the car."

Connor took a step closer to me, blocking my exit. "So, you leave Thursday, huh?"

"Yeah."

"I bet you're excited."

"Yeah."

"Chris says your family's going with you? That they're staying for a couple weeks?"

"Yeah."

"It'll be good for Abbie to get away."

"Yeah." Okay—time for a new word. "She's nervous about the flight."

"I'm sure."

I loved his eyes, so round and expressive. Looking into them now made me long for a few months ago, when he looked at me with obvious tenderness. Now he always seemed on guard. Why? Did he think if he looked at me normally, I wouldn't be able to control myself? That I'd lunge for him and confess my undying passion? Please. *I'd* broken up with *him*.

My cell phone sang from my back pocket, and I realized we'd been standing there staring at each other. Connor's face reddened and mine would've too if not for my dark skin.

"I've got to take this," I said, though if I hadn't been with them, I'd have pushed Eli's call into voice mail.

"If I don't see you before Thursday . . ." Connor didn't seem to know how to complete his thought.

I took several steps backward, toward the checkout counter. "Have a good summer, guys."

"You too," Jodi said with a big smile.

I scanned her face for signs of triumph. After all, she'd gotten what she wanted. While Jodi and Connor weren't officially dating, they appeared to be taxiing for takeoff. An afternoon movie with the family? It didn't get more "girlfriend" than that. And surely Jodi felt my spending the summer in Hawaii was the final nail in the coffin of my relationship with Connor. *I* did. Or at least I hoped it'd be the final push to me finally putting the past where it belonged—in the past.

But no matter how hard I tried to make something sinister of Jodi's smile, she seemed genuine.

Connor didn't smile, not even his crooked one. He looked like maybe he had something else to say, but he let me walk away without even a good-bye.

I turned and answered my phone with a curt, "Hey."

"We still on for tonight?" Eli asked. In the background I heard distinctive pool sounds—shrieking kids and splashing.

"Yeah, I'll be there."

"Okay. Later."

"Later."

I glanced over my shoulder as the cashier rang up my selection. Connor and Jodi's heads bent over a movie, reading the back blurb. From what I'd heard—convoluted gossip passed down from Madison—Jodi was totally smitten. She thought she and Connor could have a real future together.

Connor's feelings seemed murkier. No one knew what he thought.

I needed to look away. I couldn't get caught staring at them. But then Connor's head tilted discreetly, and he looked over his shoulder at me. His eyes shone with regret. Same as I felt in my heart but didn't admit to anyone. Not even my sister, Abbie.

I waved and forced a smile, then grabbed my movie and headed into the steamy afternoon.

Abbie looked just as sour when I got in the car as she did ten minutes ago when I got out. Maybe sourer.

"Did they have it?" she asked.

I tossed the movie to the floor. "Yep."

"It took you so long, I thought you must be trying to pick out a different one."

I ground my teeth and started the car. Each day it got harder and harder to ignore Abbie's mood. She rarely said anything blatantly mean. Instead, she sulked and sighed and draped cloaks over her insults.

I rammed the gearshift into reverse. As I waited to turn onto the busy road, Abbie noticed what I'd hoped she wouldn't.

"Isn't that Connor's car?"

I glanced at the familiar Chevy Tahoe. "Looks like it."

"Was he inside?"

I hesitated only a second. "I didn't see him."

"You're leaving for Madison's already?" Mom asked as I entered the kitchen. She stood at the counter, transferring leftover takeout into Tupperware. Even doing mundane tasks like handling discarded food, she still managed to look beautiful and regal.

"Yeah." I hitched my overnight bag higher onto my shoulder. "Where's Abbie? I wanted to say bye."

"I'm right here."

I turned to the living room. Abbie's hand waved over the back of the couch.

"I'm heading out," I said, stepping to where I could see her sprawled on her side.

"Yeah, I heard."

Owen slept beside her, turned into her body. After three months, you'd think I'd be used to seeing Abbie in a mother's role, but sometimes the surprise of it still hit me. Especially on days when she skipped makeup and braided her hair in two tails. She looked even younger than fifteen-almost-sixteen.

"See you tomorrow, pal." I stroked his silky dark hair, but he didn't stir. Looking at him, I suddenly didn't want to spend the night at Madison's, away from him. And what would he be like in two months when I returned from Hawaii? Technically we'd only spend six weeks apart since they'd be there the first two, but even just six weeks . . . He changed so often, so rapidly, I ached to think of what I might miss.

"Aren't you going?" Abbie asked.

"Right." I dropped a kiss on Owen's forehead. "Bye."

An early evening rain shower had come through, stealing away the humidity. I rolled my windows down as I drove, appreciating the fresh summer smells and cool breeze. Perfect outdoor weather—warm enough for shorts, cool enough for long sleeves as the sun set.

Lisa stood at the end of her driveway, dressed in one of her usual way-too-tight ensembles. After I'd pulled alongside the curb, she slid into the passenger seat with a mischievous grin. "You look nice."

"Same thing I've had on all day."

"Sure it is."

I rolled my eyes and stepped on the gas a little heavier than necessary. "Stop it."

"Stop what?"

"Implying I look extra nice for something. For some-*one*."

Lisa's eyes widened. "I've got no idea what you're talking about." But a smile toyed with the corners of her mouth.

"There's nothing going on with me and Eli."

"I didn't say there was."

"I leave on Thursday."

"That's like sixty-two hours from now."

I considered this. *Sixty*-two? "Seventy-two."

She blinked rapidly, the way she always did when sorting things out. "But it's three days from now. Three times twenty-four is—"

"Seventy-two."

Lisa shook her head. "Whatever. My point is, in sixty- or seventy-two hours you'll be saying good-bye to Eli. Maybe forever. Shouldn't you, like, make those hours count?"

I tightened my grip on the steering wheel. These were the moments when I missed Connor the most. He'd been a great moral compass. Lisa and Madison would have no qualms about encouraging me to make my last hours with Eli "count."

Of course, Lisa and Madison hadn't broken my heart. Score one for them.

"I'm not interested in hooking up," I said as I turned down Madison's street.

"Might be just what you need. It's good for the complexion, they say."

"Who says?"

"*Cosmo.*"

Of course. *Cosmopolitan* was the closest thing Lisa had to a Bible.

"Well, my complexion's fine." But as I pulled into Madison's driveway, I double-checked in the rearview mirror.

Lisa glanced at the in-dash clock. "Is it just me, or are we always having to wait for Madison?"

I killed the engine. "Punctuality isn't her thing."

Lisa pulled a cigarette from her purse. I might have asked her not to, but with Hawaii so close, I didn't want to bicker. "If you'd have told me six months ago that I'd be hanging out with Madison Embry . . ."

"Same here."

Lisa propped her feet up on the dashboard. I opened my mouth to tell her to move her stinky feet, but what did I care? The car would be Abbie's once I left.

"It all seems so stupid now," she said with a flick of her lighter. "Shutting Madison out of the group these last few years."

"Not much of the old group left."

She gave me a funny look. "Sure there is. It's just Jodi and Alexis who are out."

True. Jodi now spent her time with Connor and other youth group friends. I didn't know much about Alexis.

Except she didn't want to hang out with Lisa, who'd unintentionally stolen her most recent boyfriend; Madison, who'd stolen her first boyfriend; and me, whose only crime was hanging out with said girls.

"Finally," Lisa said as Madison jogged down the front steps of her modest brick house. As best she could, anyway, in her platform sandals.

Madison slipped into the seat behind Lisa. "I know I'm late. Sorry."

"We expect it," Lisa said.

In the rearview mirror, I saw Madison stick out her tongue.

"I'm sure the guys will be late too. I think Eli and John were playing disc golf," I said.

This time when I glanced in the rearview mirror, Madison grinned at me, wicked. "What?" I said flatly.

"It's just so sweet that Eli fills you in on his every move. What a good boyfriend."

Madison and Lisa cackled.

"He's *not* my boyfriend." Did they even hear me over their immature giggling? "I said, he's not my boyfriend."

"You sure spend a lot of time with him," Lisa said.

"Because we're friends, okay? We were friends for three years before we dated, and we're friends now."

"Does he know that?"

"Of course he knows."

"Is that why he kissed you?"

I hesitated, mentally replaying the kiss that had started me down this road. The familiarity of his mouth on mine, his hands in my hair, the sticky taste of rum and Coke.

"That wasn't anything," I said. "He'd recently broken

up with Jodi and I'd just broken up with Connor. It was about—"

"Attraction," Madison said.

"I was going to say 'comfort.'"

Lisa snickered. "As in Southern Comfort."

I slanted her a glare. "He may have been drinking, but I wasn't. I told you, I—"

"Gave that stuff up," the girls said along with me.

I adjusted my grip on the steering wheel and ignored their snickers. What would they say if they knew I'd been drinking too? Oh, they wouldn't really care—not like Connor would—but I'd been denying it for so long that I couldn't stand the thought of coming clean. And what really mattered was that I hadn't touched a drop since that horrible, drunken night with Eli. I cringed—okay, *one* other time. Prom night. And, okay, graduation too.

"Well, if being a good girl is what makes Eli Welling turn his head, I might just have to reform," Madison said.

I didn't answer, not quite ready to admit that I'd abandoned my fantasies of ever being a good girl.

2

"I bet they don't have Sheridan's Frozen Custard in Hawaii," Eli said as we all lounged in the bed of John's truck.

Lisa pointed her spoon at me. "Somehow I think she'll survive."

I savored an enormous bite of my caramel pretzel crunch concrete. "I don't know. I wonder if we could figure out a way to ship custard."

Sheridan's had been our hangout for the last couple summers. It was modeled after those old-timey ice cream places, where you walked up to the window to place your order, but figuring out where to eat was your responsibility. They only had a couple benches, which were always occupied except in the dead of winter. Connor and I had usually opted for the grassy slope that faced the road. These days, I usually ate with my back to the hill, to the memories.

Eli's hand clasped my bare knee. "Well, I don't feel sorry for you."

"Gee, what a great pal you are," I said, and we smiled at each other.

When Eli put his mind to it, he could give one of those mesmerizing smiles that would make a girl forget her first name. He used it on me then—the dimples, the crinkled eyes. We'd known each other for four years, and its effect on me had only slightly dulled.

"Hey, guys."

I turned away from Eli. At the end of the truck stood Connor, Jodi, and Chris, Connor's younger brother. Also probably my future brother-in-law if things between him and Abbie stayed the same.

With Connor's gaze fixed on me, I suddenly felt very aware of Eli's fingers curled around my knee, of the non-space between us. I knew how it looked. I could read it in Connor's face, and a rush of satisfaction came over me. What'd he expect? That I'd just wait around for him to figure stuff out so we could be together?

"Mind if we sit with you?" Jodi asked. She gestured to the chaos surrounding Sheridan's. "There's, like, no good place to sit."

John glanced at Eli but said, "Sure."

Connor and Chris seemed hesitant, but Jodi appeared to have no qualms about climbing in the back of the truck with me and Eli and everyone else. She smiled at me. "How was the movie?"

I saw curiosity on the faces of the others but ignored it. "Predictable. How about you guys?"

"I liked it." Jodi shrugged and turned to Connor and Chris. "Didn't you guys?"

"Yeah, it was fine," Connor said.

Chris mumbled something inaudible. It wasn't unusual for him to be so quiet, especially around people he didn't know well. But I'd rarely seen Connor so subdued.

Eli gave my leg a familiar pat. "We're all just talking about Skylar going to Hawaii. Did you guys know she leaves Thursday?"

Connor picked around his sundae and didn't seem inclined to answer. Jodi's warm smile turned polite. "Yeah. Pretty sweet."

Lisa said to Jodi, "You heard from Alexis at all?"

Jodi shook her head. "I've called her a couple times, but it's always pretty awkward. And she never calls me. Guess she's done with the whole lot of us." She smiled at something and looked at me. "You'll never guess who she's been hanging around with."

"Who?"

"I'm not even sure if you'll remember him. Aaron Robinson?"

Did she notice how stiff Connor, Eli, and I went? Eli's fingers turned wooden against my knee and Connor's bite of ice cream dangled midair, forgotten.

"Uh, kinda." I sounded surprisingly normal.

"I guess they met up at a party or something. He goes to Florida State now but is home for the summer." Jodi shrugged. "She sounded happy."

"Good. I . . . That's good, I guess."

"Not that I approve of her partying and stuff, of course."

Jodi had clearly misinterpreted my bumbling.

"Right." I had to get out of there. Had to collect my thoughts. Stupid Sheridan's for not having a public bathroom I could excuse myself to.

"Skylar, I almost forgot," Connor said. "Your iPod's in my car."

I felt like Lois Lane being rescued by Superman. If Superman were five-foot-seven with auburn hair and an absurd amount of running pants in his closet.

He jumped down from the truck and held out his hand

to help me. When his fingers clasped mine, security enveloped me. And when I landed and he released me, a fresh wave of loneliness came.

We walked away from watchful eyes, not speaking, not even glancing at each other until we reached his Tahoe. I sank to the gritty blacktop, not caring if I ruined my skirt. Connor crouched beside me, hovering in my space bubble but not touching.

"Thanks for getting me out of there," I said.

"I don't know if I need to say this or not, but I had no idea about Alexis and . . ." He wouldn't say his name. We never spoke it. "Jodi hadn't told me."

I waved away his remark. "I assumed."

"Well." Connor took a deep breath, then exhaled long and slow out his nose. "Will you call Alexis?"

"I don't know."

"It seems like it'd be a good thing for her to know. What happened, I mean."

"I know."

Images of that night spun around my head—Aaron's dark eyes, his mouth close to my ear as he whispered, "Let's find somewhere quiet," the flashing numbers of the alarm clock in the spare bedroom.

I came back to the present when Connor's fingers grazed my wet cheek.

"Sorry." I wiped away the evidence of my inner turmoil. "We should get back to the others."

"Hey." His hand caught my arm as I attempted standing. "Take your time, okay?"

I glanced in the direction of our friends. "They'll get suspicious."

19

"So? We don't owe answers to anyone sitting in the back of that truck." He tugged at his collar. "Unless you and Eli are . . ."

"No."

"Because when we showed up, it kinda looked like—"

"I don't care what it looked like. We're just friends."

Connor nodded. He wiped his wet fingertips on his athletic shorts. "What are you doing tomorrow night?"

The question threw me. I blinked at him. "What am I doing tomorrow night?"

"Yeah."

"Why?"

He shrugged. "I thought we could maybe hang out before you leave. It's been awhile."

I laughed humorlessly. Of course.

"What's so funny?" Connor asked, his face creased with a frown.

"It's just so typical 'Connor.' I'm totally unappealing to you until you see me shedding a couple tears. Suddenly you're swooping in to save the day."

His frown deepened. "It's not like that."

"What's wrong with Jodi? Is she too stable? Too sane? Doesn't need you quite as much as she used to?"

Connor's Adam's apple bobbed as he swallowed. "It's not like we broke up because I stopped loving you. I felt like I needed to be there for Jodi, and you made it perfectly clear that wasn't an option as long as we were together."

"Yeah, call me crazy. I don't like my boyfriend hanging out with girls who are so clearly after him."

"You could've trusted me," Connor said in a low voice.

"You admitted you had feelings for her."

"Not like my feelings for you."

I could no longer keep my voice cool and detached. "You chose her."

Connor gripped my hands. "I've never regretted a decision like I do that one. Please, Skylar."

"Please what?"

"Don't go to Hawaii. Or at least don't stay. Come back when Abbie and your parents do."

"You've got no right to ask me that."

"Maybe not. But I still want you to stay. I want you to be around this summer."

I pulled my hands from his. "I've been around since March. You could've done something then."

"I tried a couple times. You never wanted to talk to me."

"That's because I'm over you." I crossed my arms over my chest. "I'm over all of it."

And I turned and marched away before he could say anything to convince me otherwise.

"What's wrong?" Eli asked as I put space between us.

I finger-combed my hair as I scooted away. "We should go back to the party. Lisa and Madison will wonder where I am."

"They're big girls. I'm sure they're fine without you." He grinned and moved to close the gap between us. "I, on the other hand—"

"Stop." I pressed my hand to his chest, keeping him at a distance. "This has to stop. This thing with us."

"And it will." He brushed my cheek with the back of a crooked finger. "On Thursday."

"No. Now." I looked into his eyes. "We can't do this any-more."

Eli sighed and leaned into the backseat of the Land Rover. "Why do you always make this so complicated? I'm single. You're single. What's the problem?"

"We shouldn't be doing this." I smoothed my hair over and over, as if doing so would turn the clock back to thirty minutes ago, when I mistakenly followed Eli out here. Why did I continue to falter in this specific area? Why couldn't I say no to him?

Most days I could. Just not when I had run-ins with Connor. Then I tended to lapse into being old Skylar, the type of girl who'd make out with someone just for kicks. At least I hadn't been drinking tonight. Or did that make it worse, that I'd soberly decided to follow Eli? Or maybe not so soberly—I'd come to believe you could get drunk on pain.

Eli studied me. "Is this about Aaron?"

"No."

"I swear, when I see that guy again—"

"Don't do anything to him," I said. "He's not worth it."

Did Aaron even know what he'd done to me? And was he still doing it? Was he slipping Alexis roofies now? Or maybe he didn't need them with her.

"Maybe if you saw him again—"

"I don't want to. I just want to forget about him."

Him and everything else. I wanted to get on that plane Thursday morning and start a new life. The official line I kept giving people was that I'd come back in August before school started. I now believed this less and less. I wanted to stay there in Kapaa. What did it matter if I went to Kauai Community College versus Johnson County?

"I just think—"

But a loud rapping on the Land Rover window interrupted Eli. Both of us jumped.

"Skylar?"

Connor.

I swallowed. "Uh, what?"

"We have to talk."

I so didn't want him to see me like this, flushed and rumpled from Eli pawing me.

I glanced at Eli, who took this as an invitation to get involved. "Dude, Skylar doesn't want to talk to you, okay? Why don't you—"

"It's about Abbie."

3

Connor's face registered no emotion as Eli and I climbed out of the SUV. Eli didn't look one bit ashamed. I felt like I may as well have had the word *tramp* stamped on my forehead.

"What's wrong with Abbie?" I asked.

"Your parents called Madison's looking for you. Apparently you're spending the night at her place." Connor shot an accusatory look at Eli. "When they called me, I said you'd come over for a little bit and that we'd be right over. I'm sure they're wondering why it's taking twenty-five minutes to get from my house to yours. And why don't you have your cell on you?"

Getting in trouble with Mom and Dad didn't concern me. They couldn't do much to me now.

"What's wrong with Abbie?" I repeated.

"I'll explain in the car. We gotta go."

I didn't even glance at Eli as I left, just trotted alongside Connor to his car. Up the hill, the house party raged on. Why had I wanted to come? Or *had* I wanted to come? After my spat with Connor at Sheridan's, I hadn't much cared about my commitment to avoid parties. After all, my days of walking the straight and narrow left me hurting far worse than my *years* of partying.

"What's wrong with Abbie?" I asked yet again as I buckled my seat belt.

"Lance."

My inner claws came out like Wolverine's. "What'd he do?"

"Well, according to your parents, he came over to see Owen. I guess when Abbie wouldn't let him, he said he'd sue for partial custody."

I rolled my eyes. "He won't do that. This is, what? His third attempt to see Owen since he was born? He'll never do a thing."

"Hopefully you can convince her of that. Sounds like she's been crying hysterically for the last hour, which means Owen's crying hysterically. Your whole house is going crazy."

I gnawed at my nails, which needed to be repolished anyway. I used to keep them in perfect condition, but somewhere around March I lost my motivation. "What about Chris? Do you think he'd help?"

"He's over there now. He went as soon as your parents called me, but Abbie's asking for you."

I grimaced. "Stupid Lance." This time last year, I'd been sneaking Abbie over to his house in exchange for gas money. If I'd known what trouble it'd cause, I'd have sucked it up and paid for my own gas.

"Is your car around here somewhere?"

I shook my head. "It's at Sheridan's, but that'd take too long. Just take me home and I'll get it tomorrow or something."

I dug my cell from the bottom of my purse. Dead. Great. If I'd remembered to charge it that afternoon, maybe I'd have received the call from my parents in time to keep from following Eli out to his car. Which would mean I wouldn't be trapped in Connor's Tahoe enduring this deafening silence.

"So." Connor cleared his throat. "Eli."

"It wasn't what it looked like." I glanced at him, wondering if he believed this. If I'd seen him climbing out of the back of Jodi's Mustang, I'd have laughed in his face and then given him a piece of my mind. But Connor just kept his gaze on the road and his hands in perfect ten and two.

"You probably don't believe that," I said, when he'd been silent for too long. "But it's true."

"So you weren't making out with him?"

I opened my mouth, prepared to lie, but no sound came out.

Connor's lips thinned into a hard line. "That's what I thought."

"But we're not dating."

He snorted. "That doesn't make this better, Skylar."

I sank into my seat. Like I needed Connor to lecture me. I knew this thing with Eli and me was wrong, but if I said so, Connor would want to know why I kept doing it. He didn't understand inconsistencies, and I didn't want to explain to him how doing the right things had left my heart mutilated, but the wrong things were easy. I loved Connor, and he'd scarred me. The worst damage Eli could inflict was a bruise to my ego if he stopped coming around.

"You should be careful," Connor said, his voice tender. "You know how Eli feels about you."

I frowned. I'd expected a sermon on my virtues, not compassion for a reputed player like Eli Welling. "Eli understands the situation."

"Does he?"

"Yeah. I've made it very clear."

"Well, you making it clear doesn't mean his heart hasn't gotten involved."

"That's his problem," I said as we stopped at a red light.

Connor looked at me, his intense gaze setting my heart aflutter. "I don't like the changes I'm seeing in you."

I crossed my arms tight over my chest. "Well, come Thursday, you won't have to see them anymore."

He sighed, sounding as tired of the bickering as me. "Oh, Skylar. You know that's not what I want."

But I couldn't give him what he wanted. He liked a damsel in distress—which was why, I assumed, he didn't mind hanging around me at the moment—but I couldn't always play that role for him. And I couldn't keep losing to whoever was.

Another red light. I jumped when Connor's hand covered mine.

"No matter what does or doesn't happen between us, I still care about you."

I pried my hand away and trained my gaze out the window. If I started to cry, I didn't want Connor seeing. "Thanks for coming to get me," I said in a stiff voice.

In the reflection of the window, I saw him looking at me, his expression soft. "I'll always come get you."

Connor and I found Mom and Dad in the living room. Mom paced back and forth, Owen cradled in her arms, as she belted out "Jesus Loves the Little Children." Owen wailed much, much louder.

Dad, who juggled a full bottle, pacifier, and several blankets, turned to us with a wild expression in his eyes. "What took so long?"

"Where's Abbie?"

He nodded at the stairs.

Connor stayed on my heels as I jogged up. "You can go now," I said over my shoulder. If he heard, he didn't care.

I expected to find Abbie throwing one of her infamous fits. I assumed it'd be like the last time Lance attempted to pay Owen a visit. Abbie'd trashed her room. She tore out everything that reminded her in the least of Lance—a poster for a band they'd seen together, clothes he'd liked, a picture frame he'd bought her that I'd always thought hideous—and marched the whole lot of it to the curb with the rest of the trash waiting to be collected.

Instead, an eerie silence filled the upstairs. I froze at the top of the staircase, one hand grasping the banister. Why was it so quiet?

By the time I reached the end of the hall, I couldn't even hear Owen crying. Chris sat cross-legged on the floor of the bathroom. The door into the shower and toilet was closed.

"Catching up on your reading?" I asked in a wry voice.

He tossed the latest issue of *Jane* toward Abbie's room and used the counter to pull himself to his feet. "She stopped talking to me a half hour ago. Since the two of you took your sweet time getting over here, I didn't have much else to do."

I rapped on the door. "Abbie?"

Nothing.

"Abbie?"

Chris's words thundered. *She stopped talking to me a half hour ago.*

I yanked at the locked doorknob. "Abbie!" I thought of her parade of sour remarks, of all her emotional breakdowns since March. Of hanging my razor on the wall that morning after I'd shaved my legs. Of our first trip to Hawaii, when Abbie was four and wanted to see how long she could hold her breath in the ocean water.

I pounded on the door with my fists. "Abbie! Abbie!"

My fingers, taking on a life of their own, scrambled around the top of the doorframe. Didn't we keep the key to this stupid door up here? I had to get inside *now*. Even knowing that what I might see in there could haunt me for the rest of my life, I needed to—

"What?" Abbie demanded as she thrust open the door. "Is it too much to ask for a little privacy?"

I grabbed her close, sobbing into her copper waves.

The day's events marched through my mind as we stood there. Connor and Jodi, their heads bent together at Blockbuster. Aaron's name being spoken so casually. Connor admitting how he regretted his decision, that he still loved me. Climbing into the Land Rover with Eli. And now Abbie and those horrible images I couldn't scrub from my mind.

Abbie clung to me, her tears wetting my neck. "What if they take Owen from me?" she whispered.

"They won't."

"But what if—"

"You're his mother. And Lance is a tool."

I reluctantly let Abbie pull away. She wiped at the mascara stains beneath her eyes, smearing black granules across her temples and into her hairline. With a slight smile, she said, "Guess we scared off the boys."

I turned. Connor and Chris had gone, and it left me with

a strange sadness. I had no reason to see Connor between now and Thursday. When would I see him again? And when would I no longer care when I saw him again?

"I just want Thursday to come so we can get out of here for a little bit," Abbie said, fingers raking through her frightful hair. "I'm sick of Lance just showing up whenever he wants. Of—" She frowned and cocked her head as Owen's screeching grew loud enough to reach us here at the opposite end of the house. "How long has Owen been crying? He sounds hysterical."

She took off down the hall, her face etched with a mix of concern and urgency.

I pressed my back into the wall and glared at my reflection in the bathroom mirror. A fatigued girl stared back. Briefly this world-weary girl had been a stranger to me, but not these days. She'd been hanging around since spring break when Eli popped in for a surprise visit, a bottle of Bacardi stashed in his jacket. When I invited him in, I apparently invited her in as well. And she'd stayed.

I couldn't look at her anymore and slid to the bathroom floor. Could I leave her here and start over in Hawaii? Or would she follow me? Or, worse, hang around here until I got back and—

"Hey." Connor leaned against the doorframe and smiled his crooked smile.

I blinked at him, not wanting to feel this relief at the sight of him. "I thought you left."

He shook his head and sat beside me. Like Eli had so many hours ago at Sheridan's, Connor let his leg settle against mine. It warmed me through, thawing parts of me that had remained frosty from our breakup. Tears came.

"I don't want to do this anymore."

"You don't have to."

My mouth curled, a mixture of amusement and sadness. "You know what I'm talking about?"

"You don't want to live like this anymore."

Of course he knew. Why should I be surprised?

"I don't know how this happened. I mean, I haven't exactly done anything wrong—" Memories popped up like weeds—all three rum-and-Coke nights with Eli, a cigarette here and there with Lisa and Madison, trash-talking Jodi. Sometimes Connor.

I smoothed my skirt over my legs. "Or I haven't done anything irreversible, anyway. I just don't understand how I got on this path." After a second, I added, "It wasn't just you."

"I hope not."

But even if it wasn't "just" Connor, it was at least part Connor. He'd left to support Jodi, who'd miraculously become a Christian while trying to steal Connor from me. And because she'd needed him more, Jodi had won.

Abbie had been busy with Owen, and my parents with each other. My youth coach, Heather, was preoccupied with her new boyfriend. And the only other good influence left was Connor's mom, Amy. I just couldn't talk to her. Especially about the Eli stuff.

And without all them, I'd been left in the hands of Lisa, Madison, Eli, and John.

After my initial fall—the first rum-and-Coke night with Eli over spring break—I'd been good about avoiding tempting situations. But slowly the line of right and wrong—or maybe just my *feelings* about right and wrong—began to blur.

"Maybe it's too much about you."

I blinked at Connor. "What?"

"Your relationship with God. Maybe you're having problems because you're not really doing what he's asking."

"But he's not asking me to do anything."

"Or maybe you're not listening."

I thought of that party nearly a year ago, when God so clearly called me back to him. "He's God. When God talks, I don't think you have a choice about whether or not to listen. If he were talking, I'd hear."

Connor considered this. "My mom always explained it to me like a cell phone. You can only ignore it for so long before it needs to be plugged in. Otherwise the calls might not come through. Sure, he's God and doesn't need a charged battery or a signal or whatever analogy you want to use. And he might use a miracle sometimes to place a call, but it'd be a lot easier if you'd plug in your phone."

"I just need to get away." My mantra for the last three months. "I'll recharge, or whatever, in Kauai."

"When do you come back?" Connor asked, his hands busy in his hair.

The date on my ticket said August 13. Two months away, and it still sounded too soon. I needed more time.

I had this fantasy of sequestering myself to Hawaii for all of college. I wouldn't even come home for holidays or summers. And when I did come home after graduation, I'd blow people away. I'd be elegant and smart and on track to do something worthwhile with my life. And I'd have that quality about me—the quality I saw in Heather and Amy. Inner peace so strong it shined for all to see.

I couldn't do all that in two months.

"Skylar?"

"Sorry." I brought myself back to the present, with Skylar-the-disappointment. "August 13."

"Can I call you when you're there?"

I bit my lip so I wouldn't blurt out YES. "Why would you want to do that?"

"You know why."

"I already told you. This is over."

"It doesn't have to be."

"I don't feel the way I used to about you," I said, which was true. I used to think of Connor as someone who always looked out for my best interest. Jodi changed that. If we got back together, I'd have to figure out how to forgive him, and it was easier to stay angry. Surely I'd stop loving him soon. People were always saying high school relationships didn't last. My mom had spent the whole winter telling me that. How I hoped she was right.

I looked at Connor and saw my words had hurt him. Of course they had. They were supposed to. How else could I make it clear to him? He didn't want me. Well, he did, but only because I was messy and that's how Connor liked his girls—beautiful fixer-uppers. But when I came back from Hawaii—*if* I came back—I'd no longer need fixing up. I'd be strong, peaceful, and focused.

And over him.

4

When we arrived at Grammy and Papa's house Thursday evening, after my eyes adjusted to the dim lighting, I spotted the kitchen table. It'd been set for eight, complete with eight mismatched chairs. I quickly recalculated—two of them and four of us. Five if you counted Owen, but he didn't require a chair or a place setting.

Mom apparently noticed too. "Who else are we expecting, Mom?"

Grammy grinned. "Two of the nicest boys moved into the Whites' old house last week. Christian boys. Nice-looking ones." She jabbed her knobby elbow into my ribs and winked. "One of them is single."

"Oh, Mom," my own mother groaned.

"And if you ask me, he's the cutest one. Not sure how the other ended up with a girlfriend and Justin didn't. But he'll be perfect for our Skylar."

Behind Grammy's back, Mom mouthed, "Sorry."

"Leilani, leave the poor girl alone," Papa said as he shuffled past with a suitcase in each hand. "She probably already has a boyfriend."

"Well, she might be willing to trade him in when she gets a look at Justin."

"I don't know," Abbie said as she unbuckled Owen from his infant carrier. "Eli's pretty smokin.'"

"Eli?" Dad echoed. "Are you back with Eli?"

It took a lot of work not to glare at Abbie, which would only make me look guilty. "No."

"She totally could be, though," Abbie said, nestling sleepy Owen against her shoulder.

"Of course she could." Dad hung an arm over my shoulders. "Skylar could date whomever she wanted."

I forced a smile. "So you guys leave in how many days?"

They all laughed as if I joked.

"Go freshen up, honey." Grammy nudged me down the narrow, dark hall to the bathroom.

When I gave Mom a "help me!!" look, she followed.

She closed us into the tiny bathroom. "I'm *so* sorry," she said, inches from my face.

Grammy and Papa's house wasn't that old—Hurricane Iniki guaranteed that little in Kapaa was older than a couple decades. Yet everything was narrow or little or dark or outdated. I couldn't imagine my classy mom growing up with Grammy, who bought almost all her furniture at garage sales, then used it for another lifetime or so. Though maybe it's why every room in our house boasted a different shade of white and had that no-one-lives-here look.

"This is totally weird," I said. "Our plane barely touched down an hour ago, and already she's fixing me up?"

"I know." Mom wrung her hands together. "I should've warned you—"

"You knew about this?" I struggled to keep my voice low. You could hear everything in this house.

35

"Not *this* exactly." Mom gestured toward the kitchen. "But I could've guessed she'd do something before too long. I'm sure she's been entertaining fantasies about you falling in love with some nice island boy from a family she's known all her life. Then she thinks you'll stay here and raise your kids in a place where she can butt into everything you're doing." Mom took a deep breath.

I bit back a smile. Seeing her like this, all frazzled, made me wonder about a few months ago when she wanted to leave Dad and move Abbie and me out here. Somehow, I think we might have ended up right back in good ol' KC.

"So, what do I do?" I asked.

Mom gave me a once-over. "Brush your hair or something and we'll just deal with it tonight. I'll have a talk with Mom tomorrow." With that, she turned and abandoned me.

I *did* brush my hair, but not for what's-his-name.

When I emerged, Grammy eyed my outfit. With a furrowed brow, she asked Mom, "Are these normal things to wear on the mainland?"

Abbie turned away, but I could still hear her snickering.

I smoothed the ragged edge of my skirt—I'd gone for an island chic look and had achieved it just fine, thank you. "I'm not changing my clothes."

Mom shrugged and continued washing her hands. Grammy sighed and looked at me again, clearly disappointed.

I distracted myself with Owen, who'd woken up and was wriggling on a blanket spread on the floor of the tiny living room. I lay next to him. He smiled and rolled to his side. "Hey, pal." I maneuvered my finger for him to grasp, which never failed to make me tingle with delight. "How do you like Hawaii? Ready to get a tan?"

"Anything's better than that plane, huh, Owen?" Abbie said without looking up from her phone. She'd stretched out on the faded plaid couch.

"Who are you texting?" I asked.

"Chris. He wanted me to tell him when we arrived."

A few seconds later, her phone pinged and Abbie smiled. "Connor says to tell you hi."

I didn't answer, just focused on playing with Owen's teeny fingers. His dark eyes fixed on the rays of sunlight hitting the worn carpet.

"Should I text him hi back?"

"If I wanted to say hi to him, I'd text him myself."

"Skylar's not here," Abbie said, nice and slow as if speaking each word as she typed it. "She's getting ready for a date."

"Abbie." I groaned. "You shouldn't lie."

"If I'd sent it five minutes ago, I wouldn't have been lying."

"Yeah, well, it's not five minutes ago, now is it?"

"C'mon, let me have my fun. A little jealousy would do Connor some good."

I thought of his blank expression when Eli and I climbed out of the back of the Land Rover. It wasn't like Connor to hide his emotions. It rattled me.

Abbie's phone pinged again and she laughed a big "ha!" She resumed typing.

I wouldn't ask. I so didn't want to know.

"What now?" I asked, cringing.

"I'm explaining that we've barely stepped in the door,

but Grammy's trying to convince you to stay permanently by finding you a man."

"How do you know that?"

"I overheard you and Mom in the bathroom."

Of course. "I'm taking Owen outside."

She grinned wickedly. "Pretty eager to meet this guy, huh?"

I ignored her and stomped outside. Away from the dark house, the odor of frying fish, and my bratty little sister. Who only seemed to be in a good mood these days when picking on me. Go figure.

You couldn't see the ocean from Grammy and Papa's place. Papa said it was a twenty-minute walk to the closest beach, but I'd guess it was more like fifteen. He didn't get around so well anymore.

Owen gurgled and waved his arms as the wind blew on his face. He seemed happy, but at three and a half months old, interpreting his emotions could be tricky.

"You gonna laugh for me, Owen?" I asked, poking at his round tummy. We were all anxious for that first giggle.

I settled onto the front steps and surveyed the small, ragged yard. Our yard in Kansas came to mind, several times this size with thick, dark grass, and a strange feeling enveloped my heart. Could it be . . . ? Surely not. Surely I wasn't homesick already. I pushed away the ridiculous thought and bounced Owen on my knee.

Across the street, the screen door of a tiny yellow house opened and out stepped two guys. Probably a little older than me, but not much.

"I'd say we're looking at my date," I murmured in Owen's ear. "Which one do you think he is?"

But Owen had fixated on the swaying fronds of the palm trees and didn't offer his opinion.

As the guys came closer—dressed in nice jeans and collars—it surprised me that neither of them appeared to be Hawaiian. Instead, they looked like the same losers I'd left back home. Great.

They'd been speaking to each other in low voices as they crossed the blacktop, but when they noticed me, they became silent. On the front lawn, they stopped walking and smiled.

"Hi," I said. It seemed someone should.

"Hi," they echoed.

I stood, adjusting Owen in my arms. "Dinner's almost ready. Come on in."

I couldn't tell which of the two might be the single one, who Grammy claimed to be the better-looking of the two. They both seemed okay to me—combed hair, straight teeth. The basics.

They wordlessly followed me inside. I anticipated an awkward, silent evening. Very unlike the night I met Connor. How I hated to think about it now, but I couldn't seem to stop myself from remembering the way he'd shaken my hand, looked me in the eyes, and smiled. He'd instantly marked himself as different to me. A little strange, maybe, but different. Had that really only been last summer? It seemed like a lifetime ago.

"Oh, you're right on time!" Grammy bustled over to the door, the skirt of her muumuu swaying. "I see you've already met my Skylar and our great-grandson, Owen. And where's Abbie?" Grammy craned her neck. "Abbie, come here, dear heart."

"Just a sec," Abbie said, sounding distracted.

From where I stood, I could see she'd continued her texting in my absence. Great. She probably had me half in love with one of the speechless boys.

Grammy continued her introductions without Abbie. "That's my daughter, Teri"—Mom waved from the kitchen—"and her husband, Paul."

Dad shook each of their hands with what looked to be a firm grip. "Nice to meet you guys. Sorry, I didn't catch your names."

"Oh my lands, I completely forgot. This is Chase and Justin. And they look like brothers, but they aren't."

Other than having similar shades of brown hair, they didn't look all that similar to me. Justin stood slightly taller and had broader shoulders. He caught me looking and smiled. Not bad.

"Hey, boys," Papa said as he entered the room. "Hope you're hungry."

"You changed your shirt," Grammy said. Her face scrunched with disapproval, although his new shirt didn't look any more or less tacky than the previous.

Papa settled into his seat at the head of the table. "Owen spit up on the other."

I smoothed Owen's hair. "He's dangerous."

"He's cute," Justin said, caressing Owen's plump cheek. "How old?"

"Three and a half months."

"Everybody have a seat." Grammy shuffled toward the rickety table. "Let's see. Paul, Teri, I put you two here. Skylar, this is your glass, and Justin, why don't you sit next to her?"

Shocking. I bit back a grin, and when I glanced at Justin, I caught him doing the same. So it appeared we both understood the obvious setup taking place. At least that might make this amusing instead of painfully awkward.

"Where's Abbie?" Dad asked as we all claimed our seats.

"I'm coming!" she said from the living room.

"Put that phone down right now." Mom's singsong voice didn't fit with the command. Since Owen had arrived, Mom and Dad seemed a little lost on how to parent Abbie.

"And bring Owen's bouncy seat when you do," I added. At the sound of his name, Owen flashed me a gummy grin. "I can only balance you on my lap for so long."

Mom reached across the table. "Let Grandma take him."

"My niece is about six months old," Justin said. "My sister says there's nothing quite like being a mom."

"Does your sister live here?"

Justin opened his mouth to answer, but Grammy took it upon herself to do it for him.

"Justin's entire family lives in Cumberland, Maryland. He moved here just last week with Chase and Chase's girlfriend. They don't know anyone but us."

"I'm sure they know other people," Papa said. "They work, they go to church."

"What I meant is they don't have any *friends*. That's why it's so perfect that they'd move in just as Skylar comes to stay."

"Abigail Marie!" Dad boomed.

"Coming, coming."

"Come *now*. Everyone's waiting on you."

"Oh, don't bother her, Paul," Grammy said. When her voice took on that frosty quality, she reminded me of Mom.

Grammy and Papa had never liked Dad much. His eloping with their college-aged daughter had turned them off, no matter how rich and successful he'd turned out to be. I don't know if they knew Mom was pregnant with me when they got married. I'd only found out in January.

Abbie dropped Owen's bouncy seat to the floor space between us and slid into the empty chair beside me. Odd that Grammy hadn't flanked me with the boys to better my chances.

"Let's pray," Papa said, holding out his hands.

My stomach lurched as I remembered—they held hands when they prayed. In general, I wasn't much of a toucher, and that especially applied when it came to prayer. The few times I'd gone to youth group, they made us hold hands when we prayed and it always felt flat-out awkward to me. And with Grammy seating me next to Justin . . .

I sucked it up and laid my hand out there for him to take. As he gingerly placed his hand on top of mine, his cheeks pinkened, which I had to admit was kinda cute.

When Papa finished praying, Abbie slid her phone onto my lap. A text message from Chris filled the screen: *Have your sis call my bro. His pining is driving me crazy.*

I shoved the phone away and helped myself to the fish. "Everything smells great, Grammy," I said with a big smile.

I had only two months to get myself over Connor. I couldn't afford to be slowed down by contact with him.

By the time we got to dessert, I felt like a contender on a really lousy reality show. Justin and I said very little to each other because Grammy did all the talking for us.

"Skylar, Justin's working at Kiahuna Plantation. And he's studying hotel management."

"Justin, Skylar thinks she should go back to Kansas in August for school. I've been telling her what a wonderful education she can get at UH. Don't you agree?"

"Justin, I don't think Skylar's ever been on a surfboard. Isn't that right, honey?"

I swallowed my spoonful of chocolate pudding. "Uh, no, I haven't."

"Don't you boys surf?" Grammy asked with an innocent glance at them.

"Every morning," Chase barely managed to get out before Grammy said, "I see them head down to the beach every morning. I'm sure they wouldn't mind teaching you."

"I think learning to surf would be awesome," Abbie said as she stabbed at her pudding. She'd grown testier with each passing minute at the dinner table. What was up with her tonight?

"I'm sure we could teach both of you," Justin said.

Grammy—whose face could never conceal her emotions—seemed torn about this. I imagine she felt Abbie, being a mother, shouldn't bother with frivolous activities like surfing.

"That'd be great," I said before Grammy had the chance to say something hurtful to Abbie. But it didn't keep Abbie from stomping off to our room a few minutes later when Owen needed his diaper changed.

Mom and I exchanged a look across the table, and for about the millionth time I wondered if life would be easier or harder without me at home. But of course I couldn't just hang around the house forever because Abbie had a baby, right?

After dessert, as I carried my plate into the kitchen, Grammy practically shoved me away from the sink. "No, you go relax with our guests. You shouldn't have to work your first night here."

"We gotta get going, Mrs. Ka'aihue," Justin said with a glance at his watch. "There's this thing at the church—"

Grammy hustled over. "You're leaving already?"

"Yeah. We've got a men's group thing."

Lucky for me. Otherwise Grammy would be pushing me out the door. After a lifetime of Mom's hands-off parenting, could I handle being smothered by Grammy for the next two months? Or possibly longer?

"Nice to meet you all," Chase said. He glanced around. "Tell Abbie we said bye."

"Yeah, I will."

Chase strode to the door, seeming grateful to escape, but Justin lingered near me. "Nice meeting you."

"You too." I smiled, hoping it came across as friendly rather than flirtatious. The last thing I wanted was for Justin to think I'd somehow been involved in or encouraged this crazy setup of Grammy's. "Guess I'll be seeing you around a lot this summer."

He nodded. "We'll go surfing."

"Sounds good."

With that, he said one more thank you to Grammy and walked out the door.

"Isn't he nice?" Grammy said as I returned to the kitchen. She no longer seemed worried about me working on my first night.

I hesitated. "They both seem nice." I really, really hoped she'd drop the whole thing.

She did. For five minutes.

"Oh no!" Grammy dangled a key ring. "Skylar, it looks like Justin's left his car keys. Be a dear and run these over to him, would you?"

I bit back a groan. "Sure." I glanced at Abbie and rolled my eyes.

"Yeah, *you've* got such problems," she said.

Grammy looked awfully pleased with herself as I took the keys from her hands.

"Ten bucks says she lifted these off him," I murmured to Mom as I walked by.

Mom smiled. "No bet."

I crossed the poorly paved road to the little yellow house. Only the screen door was shut, which left me in the awkward position of either ringing the doorbell or calling inside to them. While weighing my options, Justin approached the door, presumably on his way to his church function.

"Hi," I said, feeling a little embarrassed to be standing there. I held out Justin's keys. "You left these."

"Did I?" Justin patted his pants pockets, as if his keys would be there. "Weird."

With my errand complete, I should've turned and walked back to Grammy and Papa's house. For some reason, I felt compelled to say, "Sorry about my grandma tonight. About the obvious setup."

Justin grinned. "No big deal."

"She totally sprung it on me. I swear."

"It's fine. When she invited us over, I thought it might

be something like that." Justin twirled his keys around his finger. "We really should go surfing, though. Not just because of your grandma."

"Yeah, sure," I said as I backed down the walkway. "I'll be around."

I felt him watch me walk away and tingled a little with excitement. Not about Justin necessarily, but the possibility that this could happen. That I really might get over Connor Ross.

5

After my week of sun and surf, I had no intentions of leaving Hawaii. Ever.

The breeze kicked up and I closed my eyes, savoring the warm wind on my face. If only my parents had chosen to raise us here. What a different person I'd be—laid back and stress free. And I'd know how to surf instead of looking like a bumbling moron on the board.

"There's my favorite mainlander."

I smiled and opened my eyes—Justin. "You're calling *me* a mainlander, Mister Cumberland, Maryland?"

His grin broadened. "Well, I *have* lived here a week longer than you."

"True."

Justin dropped his board and sprawled out in the sand. "The waves were amazing. You should've come with us."

I pursed my lips, thinking of my first and only day out with Justin and Chase. At youth group, I'd always felt stupid doing stuff like balloon soccer and amoeba races, but the shame of playing those games was nothing compared to my lack of talent for surfing. I couldn't stand on the board. I could barely even hang on when a wave came. And let me just say that whoever designed my adorable black-and-white two-piece didn't have surfing in mind.

"I'd like to see my nineteenth birthday, thank you very much." I lay back on the sand as well. I might regret it later, but at the moment I didn't care about getting grit in my hair. "Any big wipeouts?"

"None I want to admit." Justin blinked at the vast blue sky. "I so don't want to go to work. I should've moved somewhere rainy and depressing."

I dug my toes into the warm sand and thought about thunderstorms. I liked thunderstorms. Did they have them in Hawaii?

"You won't stay forever," Madison had told me when I said good-bye. "You need seasons."

Did I? Would endless days of sunshine and warm, salty breezes eventually drive me crazy?

"You think you'll miss seasons?" I asked Justin.

He turned to me, squinting. "The day I complain about missing winter, I give you permission to shoot me."

I smiled. "Yeah, me too. Although I like fall. And it's fun to see everything coming back to life in the spring."

"Sadly, you have to have winter to have spring."

A memory came unbidden. January—Connor and I freezing on the bleachers of the baseball field where we'd first met. My hands had tingled with cold, and I kept flexing my toes to make sure they hadn't fallen off. But then Connor had told me how beautiful I'd become inside, and it had warmed me through.

"You okay?"

"Yeah." I propped myself up and dusted the sand from my back. "Just thinking about home."

"I did too my first week," Justin said. "A lot. About my

parents, my little church, my"—he swallowed—"ex-girl-friend. But now . . ." He shrugged as best he could lying down. "This feels more like home and less like vacation. This is my real life."

And it could be mine too. If that's what I wanted.

"I've gotta get to work." He didn't move a muscle.

"That'll involve standing."

"Right." Justin eased himself off the sand. It coated his wetsuit but brushed off easily. "You around tonight?"

My heart fluttered—was he about to ask me out? "Guess so."

"Maybe I'll see you. Later."

"Later," I muttered, hating the way tears sprang to my eyes.

It's not like I was into Justin, but I could really use a distraction of some sort. As eager as I'd been to get to Hawaii, it never dawned on me that I didn't really have anything to *do* here. Other than sit around and think about life back in Kansas, the life I wanted to escape. How long would it be before I could go even five minutes without thinking of stupid Connor?

When I returned to Grammy and Papa's house almost a half hour later, I found Abbie on the scraggly front lawn. She'd donned her sunglasses and blue bikini and stretched out on a blanket in the sun. She'd spread part of it in the shade as well, where Owen lay on his back, appearing to soak in the world around him.

She propped herself up as I approached. "Justin just left for work."

"I saw him down at the beach." I dropped next to Owen. He grinned at me and pumped his legs. "Hi, pal."

"I guess I shouldn't be too surprised by all this," Abbie said in an airy voice as she settled back onto the blanket. "You've always made friends quickly with guys."

"What am I supposed to do? Ignore him?"

"Of course not."

"Then what? He lives across the street. I'm new. They're new."

She laughed. "Skylar, it was just a joke. Lighten up."

I stroked Owen's mound of soft hair. "It's not my fault two guys moved in. They could've just as easily been girls."

"I don't notice you talking to Chase very often."

"He's got a girlfriend."

The corners of Abbie's mouth quirked up.

"And what I mean by that is he's busier."

Still Abbie smiled.

I groaned. "Shut up."

"I'm not saying anything."

"Well, stop thinking what you're thinking."

"You're so touchy. If a guy like Justin noticed me, I'd be way more excited than you are." Her face flickered with a frown. "Of course, we both know my days of that are over."

"Guys notice you. Hello, Chris Ross? Your boyfriend?"

"That's because he knew me before. If he met me now, he'd never be interested." Abbie squeezed one of Owen's fat bare feet. "But that's okay."

I drew him into my lap. "Why don't you go hang at the beach for a while? I can watch Owen."

Abbie looked toward the ocean. "Yeah?"

"Sure. The sand is way nicer than this." I gestured to Grammy and Papa's lean lawn. "When does he eat again?"

"Around ten. There's a bottle in the fridge." She beamed at me as she stood. "Thanks. I'll just grab a towel and magazine and go."

Halfway to the door, she turned, her face serious. "Connor called your cell earlier. I told him you couldn't talk."

"Why'd you answer my phone?"

Her eyes narrowed. "Why'd you leave it on my bed?"

"Not so you could jabber with everyone who called."

"I think you should talk to him."

"I didn't ask your opinion."

"He can't hurt you way out here."

"Unless he called to say he's dating Jodi."

"I've seen him with Jodi. It's nothing like the way he is with you."

I had a love/hate relationship with these kinds of comments from Abbie. While nice to hear, they made resisting Connor so much harder.

When I didn't answer, Abbie lifted her shoulders in a mild shrug. "Whatever. I'm sure you know what you're doing."

Ha. More and more, it felt like I never would.

Mom and Grammy returned from their trip to the grocery store just as I laid Owen down for a nap in the room he, Abbie, and I shared.

Grammy greeted me. "Justin came by looking for you this morning. Did he find you, princess?"

I nodded.

Her eyes twinkled. "He ask you out yet?"

"Mom . . ." my mom said with a sigh.

"What? We can all tell he likes her. I don't understand what he's waiting for."

"Maybe to know her longer than a week."

"Your father asked me to marry him two months after we met. *Two months.*"

"Well, you're unusual." Mom piled mangoes in the fruit bowl. "And we're not looking to marry Skylar off this summer, okay? Keep that in mind after we're gone."

Grammy ignored this and looked around the living room, kitchen, and dining room. "Where's Abbie?" Her voice lilted with suspicion, as if Abbie could be running around getting pregnant as we stood there.

I popped a grape in my mouth. "She's at the beach."

Grammy's brow furrowed. "By herself?"

"Well, Dad and Papa are still at the golf course, you guys were at the store, and she can't take Owen. He'd be miserable in the sun."

"It's good for her to have a break," Mom said. "That was nice of you, Skylar."

Grammy's jaw clenched as if she completely disagreed, but she surprised me by keeping quiet about it.

When Grammy turned her back to put away bread, Mom winked at me and I smiled. It'd been years since Mom and I got along so well. Kinda made me sad that in a few days they'd leave, and it'd be just me, grumpy Papa, and meddling, suffocating Grammy.

6

He happened to call at a moment when I was thinking about him, missing him. That's why I answered.

"Oh. Hi," Connor said.

"Were you expecting someone else?" I asked.

"No." Pause. "I mean, kinda." Another pause. "It's been awhile since you actually answered one of my calls."

"I'm on vacation." I stretched out my legs and let the grass tickle my feet. "I've got stuff going on."

He didn't need to know that "stuff" involved sitting on my grandparents' porch, half-hoping Justin might walk over and ask me to do something so I'd stop thinking about Connor for thirty seconds.

"Right. So. How's everything going?"

"Fine."

"Just fine?"

"I mean great. Except I suck at surfing."

Connor chuckled. It sounded forced. "Must be the Midwestern girl in you."

"Must be."

Yet another pause. "Things here are good."

"Good."

"Dad, Chris, and I are playing softball on the church team. We're three and oh."

"Cool."

"I tried talking Eli into playing with us, but he hasn't shown up yet."

Why'd he bring up Eli? "Huh."

"Is now a bad time? You sound distracted."

"I'm not distracted. I just . . ." I ran my hands through my windblown hair, grateful Connor couldn't see how it aggravated me to talk to him. "I guess I don't understand what you want from me."

"What I want from you? I don't want anything."

"Everybody wants something." But I thought of the Monday before I left for Hawaii, how Connor took care of me twice and Eli just took care to proposition me.

"All I want is for us to be like we were."

"When?"

"Your choice."

"Well, we're already kinda like we were last summer. I thought you were annoying."

I thought this would offend him, but instead he laughed. "If annoyance is all you feel for me, then I'll take it. Sounds like an upgrade." He didn't wait for a response. "Cameron and Curtis miss you."

Thinking of them made me smile. I was so not a kid person, but something about those boys touched my heart. "I miss them too."

"Curtis has asked a couple times if you'll be back for his party."

"When is it?"

"July 3."

54

"You know I won't be back by then."

"I told him that. He says you will."

The thought of five-year-old—almost six-year-old—Curtis wanting me at his party tugged at my heart. Last winter, when Dad spilled about having an affair and Mom took off, the Rosses became my family. And when Connor and I broke up, not only did I lose my best friend and boyfriend, it felt like I lost a couple brothers and a set of sane parents.

"Maybe I could come back for a little bit. Abbie's birthday is around then too."

"A vacation from your vacation," Connor said. "When's her birthday?"

"The sixth. It could work out pretty nice."

"Well . . . I won't tell Curtis you're thinking about coming. I don't want to get his hopes up."

"I'll talk to my parents and let you know."

Justin's truck puttered up the road. It had such a distinct sound I could recognize it even after my short time here. He hung his hand out the window and did that Hawaiian thing that seemed to mean "aloha," "thanks," "take it easy," and a myriad of other goodwill phrases. I waved back.

"Skylar, you still there?"

"Yeah, I'm here," I said as Justin climbed out of his truck.

"I asked you about Owen. How's he doing?"

"Fine. He's getting lots of attention."

"Abbie said he screamed on the plane."

"Just for the first and last hour."

Justin crossed the street and smiled at me. I signaled I'd be off the phone soon.

"Take your time," he said in a quiet voice.

"Has he laughed yet?" Connor asked.

"Not yet. Grammy and Papa are doing everything they can to get him to. They're dying to hear it."

Across the street, Chase poked his head out the door. When he spotted Justin on our front porch, he yelled, "Still cool if I borrow your truck, dude?"

"Sure," Justin hollered back as he fished for his keys.

"Who's that?" Connor asked. Anyone would've recognized his jealousy. He rarely masked emotions. It wasn't in him to be duplicitous.

I glanced at Justin. "Neighbor."

Justin covered his mouth, as if he shouldn't have said anything, but I shook my head, assuring him it was fine.

"They must build the houses right on top of each other. He sounds close."

"Well, he's sitting here with me—"

"Oh," Connor said. "I don't want to interrupt. I'll let you go."

"Okay. Hey, tell your mom—" But the line sounded curiously quiet. I pulled the phone away from my ear to find it flashing CALL ENDED. Great.

"Sorry," Justin said. "I didn't mean to interrupt your conversation."

I sighed. "It's fine. It's just this . . ." How to describe Connor? "Just this stupid guy from back home."

"Oh." Justin fiddled with the cushion of the bench. "Is he . . . ?" He cleared his throat.

"He's an ex-boyfriend," I said, hoping to erase whatever went through Justin's mind that made his ears pinken.

"Oh. Is he the father?"

I blinked. "Who?"

Now his face bloomed crimson. "Never mind. It's none of my business."

"It's fine, I just don't get what you're asking."

"It really isn't any of my business. I just wondered if he"—Justin gestured to my cell phone—"is Owen's father. I didn't know if you guys still talked."

"Why would Connor . . ." And then it dawned on me. "You think Owen's mine?"

Now Justin blinked. "He's not?"

"No." I burst out laughing. "He's Abbie's."

"Oh." I could practically see the wheels of Justin's mind working. Thinking over events of the last week? "I guess I just saw you with him so often . . ."

"Well, he is my nephew." I grinned. "I'm pretty fond of him."

"Right." Justin's face returned to its normal shade. "Wow, I can't believe this."

"I had no idea you thought that."

"Just a misunderstanding, I guess." Justin fiddled with his shirt collar, something Connor often did when nervous. "So. Do you maybe wanna go out sometime?"

Since it was Friday and neither of us had anything going on, we skipped the formalities of "checking our schedules." He said he'd like to shower and change, and then he'd be ready. When he crossed the street, I went inside to make my grandmother extremely happy.

Grammy clapped her hands together, making her flabby arms swing. "Oh, I *knew* he liked you!"

I glanced at Mom, whose reaction had been muted.

The rule at our house had always been no dating until college. Of course Abbie had a three-month-old son and I had two ex-boyfriends, so we'd obviously gotten around it. Eli and I dated on the sly, and Connor and I got together when Mom left the first time. This made Justin the first guy I'd ever discussed with her.

"This is okay, right?" I said.

Her smile looked forced. "Of course."

Abbie emerged from our bedroom, Owen in her arms. "What's going on?"

"Justin and I are having dinner tonight."

Her smile looked weird too. "No surprise."

"I think it's wonderful." Grammy bundled me into a tight hug. "I guess it doesn't matter how long it took him to ask, just that he did."

"Grammy, I've only been here eight days."

"Still. You're a catch." She held me at arm's length and assessed my outfit. "Now, run and change before he picks you up."

I glanced at my billowy skirt and tank. "I plan on wearing this."

"On wearing *that*?" Grammy acted like I intended to wear my bathrobe and slippers.

"I think Skylar looks nice," Mom said.

"She should wear a dress." Grammy planted her hands on her hips. "Nice girls wear dresses on dates."

I looked at Abbie, hoping she'd join my side.

"I agree with Grammy. Especially for a first date," she said.

Okay—I wasn't touching another diaper between now and Thursday.

"My skirt's fine," I said through gritted teeth.

Grammy's face pinched with a frown. Mom appeared to notice. "Maybe they're right, Skylar," she said gently. "Maybe a dress would be a good idea."

Traitor.

"I'm not changing my clothes," I said as I stalked back onto the porch. "Not for anyone."

I may have been uncertain about a lot of things. Clothing was not one of them, and never again would I let somebody make me doubt how I dressed.

7

"You look really nice," Justin said as his truck begrudgingly accelerated.

I grinned. "My outfit wasn't a popular decision."

"What do you mean? What's wrong with it?"

"My grandma thought a dress would be more appropriate."

Justin glanced at his cargo shorts and polo. "I can only imagine what she thought of my choice."

"Well, *I* think you look good."

Justin's face reddened, and my heart raced. Should I not have said that? Was that stupid? I'd never done this before, been on a *real* first date. I'd known Eli for years, and we rarely did stuff just the two of us. And then Connor and I were best friends before we got together.

But Justin . . . What did I really know about him? He surfed, shared a tiny house with another guy, and most recently lived in Maryland. How did I go about learning the other stuff? The important things that made a person them. Things I knew about Connor, though I couldn't remember discussing them. Like what he'd find funny, how protective he was of his brothers, especially the little ones, and that his dad was his hero. I knew these things before the idea of dating him had crossed my mind, long before the first time we kissed—

What if Justin tries to kiss me??

The thought made me want to jump out of the truck. Was Justin the type to kiss on a first date? Would he get mad when I backed away? Did it mean something bad that I *would* back away? That I didn't want him to kiss me?

I'd spent a decent amount of time in Hawaii hoping Justin would ask me out. But now that I was here in his truck, I wanted to escape. I wanted him to turn around and take me back to Grammy and Papa's. And then I wanted to get on the first flight out of here, the first flight back to Kansas City. Back where I was comfortable. Where I belonged.

"A guy at my work said this is the best restaurant in Kapaa," Justin said as he turned on his signal. I hadn't been paying attention and now realized we'd stopped on Kuhio Highway, the main street running through Kapaa.

"It looks nice," I said as he turned into the parking lot. I folded and unfolded my hands in my lap, twisting my fingers into knots. How long would dinner take? Thirty minutes? Forty-five? Hopefully he'd take me straight home afterward.

Would dating always feel this complicated?

When Justin parked, I unbuckled my seat belt and hopped out of the truck. The fresh air eased the nausea and cooled my sweaty hands. I hoped this place had outdoor seating.

"What kinds of losers normally take you out?" Justin asked as he emerged from the truck. "The guy's supposed to get your door."

He smiled, joking, but my defenses still flared. Connor

had always gotten my door for me. Even if we were arguing. How was I supposed to know Justin planned on helping me out of the truck? He hadn't helped me get *in* the truck.

I crossed my arms over my chest so he wouldn't attempt taking my hand. "I was feeling a little carsick."

Justin frowned. "I'm sorry. Was I driving too fast?"

"No, no. It just happens sometimes."

"Maybe food will help," he said as we crossed the parking lot.

He smiled at me, kind, and I felt a rush of guilt for thinking about Connor so much. Here I was out on a date with a very nice guy and I was thinking about Connor, who'd practically forced me to break up with him because he couldn't leave Jodi alone. I needed to take a deep breath, push him out of my mind, and relax.

I started by dropping my arms to my sides. "I think the fresh air helped, because I feel better already."

"Good," Justin said. He caught my hand in his as we entered the restaurant lobby. My stomach swirled at this development, but it didn't make me want to run for the airport or anything. Good. I'd made progress.

The restaurant had a sort of washed-out Hawaiian thing going on. The decor still featured hula girls and Hawaiian flowers, but the colors were classy and muted—sand, ocean blue, dusty green. Enough to endear tourists without turning off locals.

The beautiful hostess arched quizzical eyebrows at Justin. "Two?"

"Yeah," he said.

"Right this way." She grabbed two menus and sashayed through the restaurant as if on a catwalk. Over her shoulder, she asked, "Where are you two from?" She spared me a glance. "Or do you live here?"

"We just moved here," Justin answered.

"*He* just moved here," I heard myself saying. "I live in Kansas City."

Why'd I say that? Why not let her think whatever she wanted? And I *had* been thinking about staying.

But the hostess didn't care. "Your server will be with you soon. Enjoy."

Justin furrowed his brow at me. "Your grandma said you're likely staying in Hawaii."

"I've considered it," I said. "But I'd be leaving a lot. My family, my friends."

"I understand. Believe me, I do. I just went through making that decision. But in my experience, sacrifices accompany great gains."

"I guess." I slid my menu off the table and opened it but didn't really see anything. Justin had a good point. But how did you know what to give up and what to keep? Was it weird that I still felt pangs of homesickness? Or could it all be chalked up to the fact that I'd spent my entire life in one place, and I couldn't lift myself out as easily as I'd assumed?

"Do you still get homesick?" I asked.

Justin nodded. "But it's getting better." When he smiled at me, my stomach flip-flopped in that good, new-crush kind of way. "I'm really glad you agreed to dinner tonight. I've had a tough time finding fun, beautiful, and interesting Christian girls I want to spend time with."

And that's when the reality of the situation hit me.

Justin didn't know I'd been a Christian for only a year.

And that for a lot of that time, I hadn't been a very good one.

He didn't know about Aaron.

He didn't know about Eli.

He didn't know I used to smoke, that rum and Coke was my danger drink, and that I'd dated two of my best friend's ex-boyfriends. He wasn't there when I crashed my mom's car sophomore year or when I got drunk two Valentine's Days ago and called Alexis skanky. When I was with Justin, those parts of me, those events, didn't have to exist.

A year ago, I'd committed to reinventing myself. To becoming a new Skylar. For a little while, I felt like I'd taken off, like I was doing better, only to crash and burn during the spring. Maybe this was what it'd take to become a new me, a different me. Maybe I could really do it if I could start over someplace where no one knew a thing about me. Yeah, the idea of never going home scared me a little, but Justin's warm, dark eyes made me want to stick with this. Made me want to see who I could be with a clean slate.

I smiled back at him. "I'm glad you asked me."

"And she just ignored you after that?" I asked, taking a big bite of my heavenly hana ice cream—chocolate ice cream with marshmallows, white-chocolate-covered macadamia nuts, and dark-chocolate-covered almonds. Maybe I could survive without Sheridan's.

"It was like I didn't even exist."

I shook my head. "Chicks."

Justin grinned. He had a great smile. "They're not all bad."

"But still. Leaves you at a dance, and then doesn't even apologize? That's cold."

Justin licked his disgusting Kona coffee ice cream cone. "You should feel honored. I rarely tell anyone that story. It's embarrassing."

"Yeah, for her."

He smiled again. "I knew I liked you."

We walked quietly along the lamp-lit Kuhio Highway. While the date had started off rocky, it turned into a pretty good one. We'd skipped the overpriced dessert menu at the restaurant, did a little shopping in downtown Kapaa until the stores closed, then walked down to Lappert's for ice cream. Now, on the walk back to the car, I felt almost relaxed.

Then Justin looked at me in a way that sent my stomach swirling again. I had at least learned, as the night progressed, to pause my eating and resume when the butterflies subsided. Same as Abbie had done when she was pregnant. Which reminded me . . .

"I still can't believe you thought Owen was mine."

"You know, it's funny." Justin stuck his free hand in his pocket. "I've been thinking about that all night, and there's something I can't explain away."

"What?" I asked.

"Remember yesterday morning when I came and found you at the beach?"

I nodded.

"Well, when I went back home to change, Abbie was in the front yard with Owen. I went over to say hello and we talked for a couple minutes. And—" Justin reddened. I loved that. "Well, I was trying to find out information about Owen's father, so I said, 'I don't think he looks much like

Skylar.' Abbie said, 'You don't?' And I said, 'Do you think he looks like her or the father?' Abbie said, 'Most people think he looks like me.'"

"And are we ever grateful," I said. "The last thing she needed was Owen turning out just like Lance."

"So, anyway, I said, 'I bet that's frustrating. People probably think he's yours.' And now that I think about it, Abbie did give me sort of a weird look. But she said, 'Yeah, it's annoying.' And then she went on to say a bunch of stuff like she felt sorry for you because Owen took up so much of your time and that all your friends had deserted you, and that's why you're thinking about staying in Hawaii permanently."

I gaped at him. "She didn't."

He looked uncomfortable. "She definitely wanted me to think Owen was yours. I even told her how nice it was that she'd babysit so you could have some time on the beach."

My head ached from grinding my teeth. "What'd she say?"

Justin swallowed. "That it'd been really hard on you to have a baby so young."

8

"Oh my gosh, relax," Abbie said.

"Relax?" I hissed. I wanted to yell but couldn't with Owen snoozing in his Pack 'n Play in the corner of our room. "You told Justin that Owen's mine."

"I was just having some fun. I knew it'd sort itself out. At the very least, he'd figure it out when I left on Thursday and took Owen with me."

I stared at her—her unrepentant eyes, the amused curl of her mouth. I had no response, at least not one I'd be comfortable saying with Owen in the room. I marched out, letting the door slam behind me. Then winced. Yeah, I was mad, but waking up Owen seemed unnecessarily mean. Fortunately, no cries came from our room.

I stalked through the dark, silent house and out the front door. Just six more days and she'd be gone. I couldn't wait.

I flopped onto the padded porch bench and curled my knees to my chest. Across the street, in the little yellow house, lights blazed. Chase's girlfriend was there. Justin had invited me over as well, but I'd been too irritated with Abbie to even consider it. Maybe I should go over there now.

A few minutes later, when Grammy and Papa's screen door opened, I hadn't yet decided.

Abbie sat beside me. She drew her knees up as well, then returned her feet to the floor. Then crossed her legs, then uncrossed. She sighed. "I guess I was feeling a little jealous about Justin. We all knew it was coming, him asking you out, and I just . . ." Another sigh. "It's never gonna be like that for me again."

I frowned. "You've got Chris."

"I know. But it's so complicated. I'm not even sixteen. I should be able to go on dates with my boyfriend. I shouldn't have stretch marks. I shouldn't—" Abbie bit her lip as tears rolled down her face. I stretched my arm around her shoulders and she leaned into me. "I shouldn't complain, I know. Owen's awesome. I'm crazy about him. I just . . ."

"I know," I said.

She righted herself, still sniffling. "Sorry I ruined things for you."

"You didn't ruin anything. He still asked me out. And this way, when people ask how we met, we have a cute story."

"So you like him?"

"We had a lot of fun."

She wiped her nose with the back of her hand. "You like him more than Connor?"

I hesitated. "I can't compare them. Connor . . ."

There were so many ways to finish that sentence. Connor was my first love. He'd taken care of me when I'd been an afterthought to everyone else. His family had practically adopted me. That couldn't be erased by one date.

"Connor's special," Abbie finished for me.

I frowned. I didn't want it phrased that way. "Connor hurt me. Justin hasn't."

"Give it time."

I snorted. "So cynical."

"Not cynical, just honest." Abbie shrugged. "Even the best guy's going to screw up every once in a while. You're in love with Connor. He's in love with you. I think you should put this whole Jodi mess behind you and make up."

I drew in a ragged breath. I hated talking about this. "I told Connor she was after him. He didn't listen."

"He regrets that now."

"But what—" I stopped and looked at her. "Do you two talk about me?"

Abbie shrugged.

"Well, don't. Or at least when you do, pretend to be on my side."

"Oh, I do." Abbie grinned. "Believe me, I let him have it. But truthfully, I think it's time to let it go and get on with it. Forgive him."

I sighed and looked across the street at Justin's inviting house.

Abbie followed my gaze. "Oh, come on. You just met the guy."

"Exactly." I leaned back on the bench. "It's nice. Having a clean slate."

I felt her looking at me. "Connor doesn't care about your past, Skylar. He's proven that by now."

"Doesn't it ever feel weird with you and Chris? He's lived this perfect, saintly life and—"

"And I have a baby? It's not that I don't get what you're feeling, because I do. But wouldn't it be stupid of me to throw away my relationship with Chris just because he's such a good guy?" Before I could answer, Abbie continued. "Stop making excuses. You're being a huge chicken, and you know it."

I forced a laugh. "How am I being a chicken?"

"I know you're thinking about staying in Hawaii longer than the summer. That's being a chicken."

"That's really none of your—"

"Business? Well, last winter when you told me *I* was being a chicken for planning to move to Hawaii, it wasn't any of your business either."

I swallowed. "That's different. You'd have been leaving school. But I'm supposed to be going away to college anyway—"

"And if you had a college you wanted to go to, that'd be one thing. You don't. You want to get away from Connor. You're running away."

I clamped my mouth shut. She made too much sense for me to argue.

"Just leave me alone, Abbie," I said as tears squeezed from the corners of my eyes.

And miraculously, she did.

"Skylar." A male voice. Vaguely familiar. Again: "Skylar." Something poked my side. "Skylar, wake up."

I cracked open my eyes to find Justin squatted next to me. Where on earth . . . ?

I winced as I sat and took in my surroundings—the front porch. From the ache of my muscles, I'd spent the night here on the bench. I vaguely recalled lying down.

"What time is it?" I asked.

"A little after five. I was getting in my truck to go to work and saw what turned out to be your cell phone blinking. And then I noticed you. Everything okay?"

I still had on my makeup and date clothes. I'd come home from our date and marched through the dark house straight to the bedroom to yell at Abbie. I hadn't even brushed my teeth—ew.

"Yeah, I just . . ." I massaged my neck as I searched for an appropriate answer. I really didn't want to relive my argument with Abbie. "I guess I just fell asleep."

"So I know I'm supposed to give it a couple days or whatever"—Justin shifted and his knees cracked—"but Chase and Kelli are going out tonight and asked if we want to come along."

"Kelli's Chase's girlfriend?" It all seemed foggy at the moment.

"Yeah. I think you'd really like her. I don't know what we're doing yet. They mentioned bowling, which they're both way into." Justin shrugged. "I know that sounds kinda lame."

"No, it sounds fine." I smoothed my knotted hair.

"I gotta go. I get off around three today. I'll come over after I shower and stuff. Cool?"

"Yeah."

He squeezed my knee as he stood. "See you then."

I dragged myself off the bench, trudged through the dark house once again, and collapsed into bed beside Abbie.

"No," Dad said in a flat voice.

"No?" I repeated. "You're not even going to think about it?"

"If you want to come home with us on Thursday, that's one thing, but I won't have you constantly flying back and forth from Hawaii to home."

"One trip isn't constantly."

"If I say yes to this trip, then what about in a month when it's Connor's birthday?"

"Connor's birthday is in December."

Dad spread guava jelly on his toast. "Do you see my point or not? You decided you needed time away, that you wanted to spend the summer in Hawaii. Now you need to live with that decision."

I chewed on my lip. "But you just said I could go home on Thursday if I wanted."

"Completely different."

"How?"

"That's making a choice. I'm saying no to you . . ." Dad waved his hand, searching for the right word. "Dibble-dabbling around."

"Dibble-dabbling?"

"Yes. Either you choose to come home and deal with everything, or you choose to stay here through the summer and get a little space. No in-between stuff."

A new voice entered the conversation: "Skylar, dearest, can I make you some French toast?"

Grammy stood in the kitchen, her wet hair wrapped in curlers and her floral bathrobe cinched around her waist. How long had she been standing there? I'd purposefully chosen to have this conversation with Dad while she showered.

"No, I ate already." I nudged my empty cereal bowl, as if I needed proof. "Thanks."

"Cereal's not a real breakfast." Grammy pulled eggs from the fridge.

I glanced at Dad, hoping he'd help me out. He gazed

out the window and seemed not to hear us. "I eat cereal all the time. It's fine."

"Not in this house it isn't."

"Grammy, really, it's fine."

"Hush. Now go take your shower, and by the time you get out, I'll have some nice French toast all fixed for you."

I gave Dad one last "help me" look, which he didn't notice, and backed away from the table. I moved toward the sink to rinse my bowl.

"Oh, just leave that there, dear heart. I'll take care of it."

"Okay, thanks." I left my bowl and shuffled down the hall.

As I knelt at my suitcase in the bedroom, gathering clothes for the day, Dad and Grammy's conversation floated through the vent.

"Don't try forcing her to return to Kansas City," Grammy said as I leaned closer.

"I'm not." Dad sounded calm and collected. "But I've no intentions of shuttling her back and forth all the time. If you and Kelani choose to, that's your business."

"Skylar's very fragile right now, and we're willing to give her all the attention she needs. What about you, Paul? Are you willing? Or do you still think that stupid company matters more than your own family?"

Was I fragile? I'd always thought of myself as strong, but the last couple months had proven otherwise. The parties. The drinking. Eli. One setback and I'd fallen right into my old lifestyle. How weak did that make me?

"My daughter's not fragile," Dad said in a stern voice I knew well. "Yes, she's hit a rough patch, but I know Skylar. Once she gets her footing, she'll come back even stronger.

She doesn't need me telling her what to do. And the last thing she needs is you smothering her, trying to manufacture a life for her here in Hawaii. Trying to make up for what happened with Teri."

Grammy didn't respond, or if she did, I couldn't hear it over my crying.

9

I hoped a quiet afternoon of bumming around the beach would help me sort out my to-return-to-Kansas or to-not-return issue. Without Abbie's sullenness, Owen's screeching, or the strange tension between my parents and grandparents, surely I could sort out the next couple years of my life.

So when my jingling cell phone pulled me away from my deep thoughts, I nearly ignored it. But I could at least check the caller ID. Heather. It'd been weeks since I talked to her. I used to see her every Saturday, back when we had sewing dates over at her tiny cottage of a house.

Heather and my drifting apart wasn't really anybody's fault. It certainly hadn't helped our relationship that when I broke up with Connor, she'd just started dating a doctor from her work and was in that whole moony, new-love phase. I'd been happy to put a little space between us. To have one less person asking questions about my behavior.

Seeing her name on the caller ID made me nostalgic. This was, in fact, Saturday. I'd normally have been at her house.

I popped open my phone. "Hey, Heather."

"Hey, girl!" Heather blasted me with enthusiasm. "What's going on?"

I resettled in my lounge chair and tipped my face to the sun. "Just hanging out. What about you?"

"Brent proposed!"

I sat up. "He proposed?"

"Yes! He took me out to dinner at Planet Sub last night—long story, don't ask. But anyway, he proposed! Got down on one knee and everything! And I was stunned. I mean, I just sat there gaping at him. And everyone cheered. It was surreal. I'm sure they all thought he was a total cheapskate proposing at Planet Sub, but I couldn't very well go into the whole story with them . . ."

I smiled as Heather rattled on. A right she'd earned. Heather had been waiting a very long time for the right guy to come along. And now it appeared he finally had.

Ugh—*appeared* he finally had? Old, cynical Skylar talked like that, but not me. Brent *was* the right guy for Heather.

"When's the wedding?" I asked as Heather wound down her story. "Or do you know yet?"

"August 1."

"August?"

I apparently said this pretty loud—a nearby tourist family turned to look at me, their children pausing mid–sand castle. I ignored them.

"I know it's a little hasty—"

"A little? That's like . . ." I couldn't do the math quickly enough. "Really soon."

"Six weeks. Which is nuts, I know, but it's also pretty romantic. We were going to wait and do a holiday wedding, but his sister's getting married then and it's this huge, formal affair where, like, everybody except the president is expected. Then we found out my sister, Lane, is leaving in the middle of August for Africa. She'll be there a whole year and I don't want to have it without her, but I don't want to wait that long either. So we thought if we kept it small, like just family and close friends, we could get away with an outdoor wedding at Loose Park. Wouldn't that be gorgeous? In the rose garden—"

"I can't come." The thought of not being there brought tears to my eyes.

"What do you mean you can't come?"

"I'm in Hawaii until the thirteenth."

"I thought you came back this Thursday."

"No, just my family."

"Well . . ." The joy had drained out of Heather's voice. "Well, that sucks. I'd really counted on you being here. I thought we could have the best time making my dress together—"

My heart wrenched with pain. "Your wedding dress?"

"Yeah. I was thinking something simple since it'll be outdoors, but something different too. Like maybe a sweet-heart-style top, but then a flowy, kind of casual skirt."

My head swam with options. A cotton dress, brilliant white with a subtle rose pattern. Or maybe with roses sewn along the skirt hem. An asymmetrical skirt hem.

My fingers ached for my machine.

"It'd be amazing," I said, my voice thick.

"Maybe you could fly back for the wedding."

I thought of my dad that morning and knew it was out of the question. "Maybe."

"Oh, I hope so! It just wouldn't be the same without you."

Justin lumbered down the beach. It must be later than I thought, since he'd already changed out of work clothes into board shorts and a T-shirt. "Mind if I call you back a little later? I need to go."

"That's fine. Call whenever."

"Okay. Wait, Heather?"

"Yeah?"

"Congratulations. I'm really happy for you."

I could hear her smile. "Thanks, Skylar. Bye."

"Who are we happy for?" Justin asked as he settled into the sand beside me.

I clicked my phone shut. "My friend Heather. She just got engaged."

"Cool." He tipped his face into the wind. "I don't think I'll ever get used to how beautiful it is here."

That was it? He couldn't muster up any more excitement? Of course, he didn't know Heather. If he'd told me some random chick from Cumberland was getting married, I wouldn't have much to say either. But I'd at least ask when the wedding was or how they met. Something to show interest.

"So, Chase and I decided to make dinner for you girls. You eat meat? We're gonna grill steaks."

"Steak sounds great," I said as I pulled on my tank.

"If you don't eat meat, we can grill you some veggies or something. Kelli's a vegetarian and we're already grilling them for her, so it'd be no problem."

"I eat meat." If I sounded slightly annoyed, it's because I was. I mean, I said it sounded great. I wouldn't have said that if I didn't eat meat.

"Some girls just agree so they won't seem difficult."

"Well, I don't mind being difficult."

Justin grinned. "You ready to go?"

"Yeah, sure."

As we gathered up my beach stuff, my phone pinged with a message. I opened it to see a picture from Heather. Her thin, graceful finger sporting a healthy-sized diamond.

Wow, I texted back. *Brent have any brothers?*

After I sent it, I turned my phone to Justin to show him the picture. "Look. Isn't it pretty?"

"Mm-hmm." He sounded like he couldn't care less. Of course, he was a guy.

With only a moment's thought, I forwarded the picture to Connor with a simple, *Heather's engaged.*

"Can you walk and text?" Justin asked, hoisting my beach chair over one arm. "I'm hungry."

"All done." I tucked my phone in my back pocket and forged the sand alongside Justin. "How was work?"

"Fine. Nothing out of the ordinary. Hey, you want a job at the hotel? Because I could maybe talk to someone for you."

"Thanks, but no. I don't need one."

Justin turned to me, his forehead wrinkled. "You don't need a job?"

"No."

"How nice," he said wryly.

I toyed with the ends of my hair. I'd never had a job before, never needed one, but nobody had ever made me feel bad about it.

"I doubt anyone will want to hire me for just a couple months." As if otherwise I'd be out there pounding the pavement right now.

The creases in Justin's forehead deepened. "You said you might stay for school."

"Yeah, I *might*." My ringing cell phone interrupted. I glanced at the display—Connor—and pushed him into voice mail. "I haven't made up my mind yet."

"Why not?"

"Well, it's a big decision."

"If you're not staying"—Justin stopped walking and faced me—"then what are you doing with me?"

The sun hung golden behind him, silhouetting him against the blue sky. It made it impossible to read his expression.

"What do you mean?"

"I mean, what's the point of us starting up something if you're leaving in August?"

Like hanging together was pointless if I didn't eventually have a ring on my finger? Hello, what about just having fun?

"We can't just hang out?" I asked, shifting so I could see his face better.

"We can, I just . . ." He took a deep breath, his gaze intense on my face. "Oh, why not just tell you. I really like you, okay? You're sweet and fun and beautiful, and I had a great time last night. But I don't do summer flings. I don't want to get too involved if you're leaving."

"I don't know if I can just pick up and leave Kansas City."

"Why not?"

My phone chimed with a voice mail. Connor, presumably.

"Well, there's Abbie and Owen to consider."

80

Justin nodded as if thinking about this. "I don't mean this the way it's potentially going to come out, but why should Abbie get consideration above what *you* want? If you can't leave home now, if you feel too tied down, when *will* you be able to leave?"

A good point.

"I guess you're right." I resumed walking. The conversation had gotten a little too intense, too pointed, for my liking.

"I know it's hard to make a change," Justin said, walking with me. "But you made the decision to move to Hawaii, and you should stick with it."

Before I came, I didn't have a doubt in my mind that I should be here in Kauai. But now there seemed a thousand reasons to go back. And not just in two months, but on Thursday with the rest of my family. But how could I do that? How could I go home and just give up on reinventing myself?

The counterquestions came unbidden. How could I give up watching Owen grow up? Seeing Heather get married? Leave my sister to fend for herself when I'd said I'd be there?

My phone chirped again and I silenced it. "I just don't know what's right."

I didn't realize I'd spoken it out loud until Justin said, "I think you know you're supposed to be here. You're just not ready to admit it."

But if that was true, why did it aggravate me to hear him say so?

"So, I've seen your nephew outside," Kelli said. "He's darling."

"Isn't he? We're all crazy about him."

"I love babies." She sighed. "Chase thinks it's weird."

"They don't do anything," Chase said absently. It sounded like an old argument.

Kelli rolled her eyes at me, and I smiled. She reminded me a lot of Heather, very sweet and confident. She'd moved to Hawaii with the guys and lived by herself in what she described as a teeny-tiny shoebox of an apartment. Kelli seemed hungry for friendship, which suited me fine. I'd never had a Christian friend my age. Well, Justin, Chase, and Kelli were two years older, but basically my age.

We'd long ago finished dinner, and now the four of us sat on cheap white chairs on the guys' rickety wooden patio, watching the sun set. My friends back home would've busted out the liquor at a moment like this, but my new friends seemed content with Cokes as they entertained me with stories of back home. Well, "entertained" wasn't the best word. I had a tough time following some of the stories but appreciated their efforts to include me. They seemed eager to accept me as a new member in their group, and with the warm breeze on my face and no pressures to light up or doctor my Coke, joining them sounded good to me as well.

I pushed back from the table. "Where's the bathroom?"

"Down the hall and on the right," Justin said.

"And don't worry," Kelli said. "It's clean. I made sure."

I wound my way through the guys' house, which was small and creaky like my grandparents', only with sparse furniture and excessive electronics. They had no couch or dining room table, but there were two stereo systems and a TV that took up nearly an entire wall.

As Kelli promised, I found the bathroom clean. I washed my hands with off-brand soap that smelled of gummy bears and dried them on what had clearly been one of their mom's old dish towels—red gingham printed with green peppers. Soon, this might be my life too—skimping on soap and using castaway towels. Maybe living with Kelli. Working a lousy job or two.

A thrill ran up my spine as my hands grew clammy with fear. How could I be so conflicted about the idea of moving out on my own? A year ago, when my life was warring parents and a pesky little sister, I'd yearned for this moment. Now that it had arrived, would I be brave enough to seize it?

Walking through the house to the back porch, I heard the muffled sound of my cell phone beeping from my beach bag, indicating a message. I thought I'd silenced it back at the beach.

When I pulled out my phone, I found I'd missed another call from Connor and now had two voice mails. I couldn't resist finding out why he'd called twice.

As I waited for my password to register, Kelli's loud, clear laugh reached me. Why was I wasting time checking voice mail? I should be out on the patio enjoying my new friends.

I moved my finger to disconnect the call, but stopped when Connor's excited voice burst in my ear. "I can't believe you sent me such awesome news in a text message! I'm so happy for Heather. And Brent seems like a really nice guy. You like him, right? I think you said you did, but I can't remember now. Anyway . . . thanks for letting me know. Talk to you later. Bye."

83

Thankfully no one could see me smiling. Or saving the message when it made so much more sense to just delete it.

Connor's voice came on the line again, this time more subdued. "Hey . . . I hoped you'd pick up, but I probably should've expected voice mail. Anyway, I thought I should apologize for yesterday when I hung up on you. I heard that guy and just . . . And it's stupid because you told me when you left that we were over, so I had some idea that you'd be moving on, but . . . I don't know. I sound stupid. All I wanted to say is I'm sorry for reacting the way I did." He paused and my breath caught. "I miss you, Skylar. Hope to see you soon."

I snapped shut my phone, blinking away the tears blurring my vision. How could I even think of going back home? I'd just wind up back together with Connor. Or falling back into the trap I had this spring—Eli and parties and so on. I could not let that happen again.

"Hey, Skylar, everything okay?" Justin called through the screen.

I shoved my phone into my back pocket, along with my cozy feelings for Connor. "Everything's fine."

I rejoined my new friends on the patio, all smiles and chatter. They didn't know to look for the tick in my left eye to see if I was emotional. Or the bridge of my nose creasing when I fought back tears. They didn't know me, but they wanted to, and I wanted them to. Or at least the things I didn't mind sharing.

And with their help, I could reinvent Skylar Hoyt.

10

"You, like, have to come back," Lisa said with a loud pop of her gum. "There's nothing to do here."

"Yeah, sounds great," I said as I applied mascara. Juggling my cell phone, compact, and Lash Factor brought a pang of nostalgia for the spacious vanity in Abbie's and my bathroom. At least in three days I wouldn't be sharing Grammy and Papa's half bath with my entire family.

"Oh, has Madison told you? Eli's hooked up with this really obnoxious girl. She laughs at everything he says. I'm not even kidding."

I forced myself to giggle along with her. I'd hate for Lisa to suspect I felt strange about Eli replacing me. Not that I hadn't expected it. We hadn't talked since that night Connor came to get me because of Abbie's meltdown. Which, now that I thought about it, really irked me. Eli hadn't even cared enough to see what the deal was with Abbie and if she was okay. How insulting.

"Oh, and . . ." Lisa's tone turned serious. "I'm pretty sure Connor and Jodi are official now."

All thoughts of Eli evaporated. "Why do you say that?"

"Madison and I were at Starbucks yesterday, and they were there too."

My heart rate returned to normal. "Coffee at Starbucks doesn't equal dating."

"I was definitely picking up a vibe."

"What kind of vibe?"

"Like a dating vibe."

I rolled my eyes at my reflection. "Were they, like, holding hands or anything?"

"No, but you know how they are. They're practically Puritans."

I thought of Connor's mouth warm against mine. There'd been passion, but an understanding that it belonged to us and we'd stay in control.

"They're not Puritans." I snapped shut my mirror. "They just believe in self-restraint."

"Whatever. Tell me about Hawaii. I have to vacation vicariously."

"Hawaii's . . . great."

"Well, that's convincing."

"No, it is. It's beautiful. And there's this guy who—"

Abbie entered our room, bringing Owen and a ripe-smelling diaper.

"A guy who what?" Lisa asked. "Did you meet a guy, Skylar Lynn Hoyt? No surprise. What's he like? Is he a native? Because they're so hot."

"I'll call you back later," I said and hung up.

"Bet you'll be glad when we leave and you can have a private conversation," Abbie said as she stretched Owen out on the floor. "I'm *so* ready to get away from here. I don't know how I'm going to put up with Grammy until Thursday. How will you do it all summer? Or more?"

Before I could answer, Abbie turned her head. "You

hear that?" She scooted closer to the vent. "It's Mom and Grammy."

"Abbie, maybe we shouldn't—"

"They're talking about you."

I crouched beside Abbie just in time to hear Mom say, "Skylar wanting to stay here has nothing to do with me and Paul."

"You're lying to yourself," Grammy said. "The only time children want to leave home is when there's something wrong."

"She's eighteen. She starts college this fall. It's a perfectly normal time for a child to leave the house."

"What about Abbie? She wants to stay."

Abbie gaped at me. "I so do *not*."

"Shh," I said.

"No, Mom. Abbie used to want to come here, back when Paul and I were having problems. But she's fine now, and she's happy in Kansas."

"Until next time Paul hurts you," Grammy said, her voice soft. Or maybe it just seemed that way because it filtered through the vent. "He always seems to hurt you."

"That's life. That's marriage. I've hurt him too. Haven't you and Dad hurt each other?"

"Never like this. Never where we had to get counseling."

"There's nothing wrong with us getting counseling," Mom said. "At least we're willing to work things out. Not just bury our problems and hope they disappear."

"I don't know what you're implying, Teri, but I don't like it."

"Then I think you *do* know what I'm implying." The unmistakable sound of a chair sliding against the linoleum. "Skylar staying is her business and me going home is mine. Don't try making either of them yours."

A few seconds later, the front door slammed.

We stared at the vent until Owen fussed and Abbie had to tend to him.

"No Justin today?"

I turned and found Papa seated on the patio bench, hands occupied with an electronic poker game.

"He's working." I took a seat next to Papa. Mom, Dad, Abbie, and I were headed down to the beach, but it looked like I was the only one ready.

"Seems like a nice guy, Justin."

"Yeah, he does."

"'Course, that Connor fellow sounds nice too."

When I looked at him with wide eyes, Papa smiled. "That sister of yours likes to talk."

"Great," I muttered and burrowed my back into the bench cushion.

We sat in our normal uncomfortable silence. Shouldn't I know how to talk to my own grandfather? I wanted to say something, to get to know him, but didn't know how. He seemed to have the same problem with me.

Until now.

He laid down his poker game. "Your mother—" He frowned, seemed to reconsider his words, and started again. "Your mother and I have never gotten along. I knew how to handle her until she was about two, but after that we never communicated well. Same for her and Leilani. Teri was always our independent girl. Your aunt Sylvie wanted us involved in every detail of her life, but not Teri. She wanted to be alone, wanted to do it herself, and begrudged us for wanting to be involved." Papa sighed. "And maybe we were too controlling. I don't know anymore."

I thought of my mom, who'd erred on the side of being too hands-off. What would she have to say about this conversation?

"Teri practically skipped onto the plane the day she left for college." Papa turned to me, his eyes weary and sad. When I touched his hand, he brightened slightly. "You look so much like her. And you should understand that's what's so difficult for your grandma. When she sees you, she sees an opportunity for a do-over. And I think when your mother's encouraging you to leave Kansas City, it's because she did something very similar at your age and doesn't want to admit it might not have been the right choice."

Papa fixed me with a hard look. "But you're not your mom. And you can't be responsible for fixing what went wrong so many years ago. You need to follow the path the Lord set out for you and you alone."

"But I don't know what that is," I said. "I don't know what he wants."

Papa frowned. "Which will take more courage? More trust? Which will grow your character? Because your character is his primary concern."

The screen door squealed as Mom and Dad emerged from the house. "Abbie's not out here?" Mom asked.

"Nope." I glanced at Papa, finding him once again absorbed by his poker game, as if our conversation had never happened. "You want to come to the beach with us, Papa?" I asked.

"No thanks." He didn't even look up.

I caught Mom rolling her eyes at Dad. Why couldn't Papa have said everything to Mom that he'd said to me? Why did people do that? Act like they didn't care while inside they ached all over? Stupid pride, that's all it was. Not wanting to admit how badly they'd been hurt. As if keeping people at bay could fix anything.

Abbie danced out the door. "He's asleep. Let's go." She planted a kiss on Papa's smooth cheek. "I gave Grammy all the instructions so you won't have to do anything."

"You're an angel," Papa said. "Have a nice time."

As the four of us walked down the blacktop road, I realized it was the first time it'd been just us—no Owen, no one else—in a very long time. Perhaps since March.

Maybe Mom had just realized the same thing, because she said, "It's quiet without Owen. I miss him."

"Any more laughing?" Dad asked Abbie.

"Any *more* laughing?" I said. "Did Owen laugh?"

The three of them frowned at me. Dad said, "It must've happened yesterday when you were at lunch with Justin."

I gave Abbie an accusatory look. "And no one told me?"

"I didn't think to. Sorry."

My heart felt heavy. "I can't believe I missed hearing him laugh the first time."

"You should get used to it," Abbie said, her voice flippant.

"Let's not talk like that," Mom said. "Let's just enjoy our time."

And I really tried, but Abbie's words taunted me through-out our walk. I didn't want to miss everything with Owen. His first bites of food, crawling, hearing his attempts to say my name. Would he even know me if I came home in August? Or would he scream and cry when Abbie left him with me, same as he did with the strangers in the church nursery?

"Are you crying?" Abbie asked.

I blinked in the glaring sunlight and found my family watching me. "I want to go home with you on Thursday."

Mom pushed her sunglasses off her face. "You *what*?"

"I don't want to miss everything."

She frowned at this. "Skylar, you need to think this through. You don't want to make a rash decision just be-cause you're scared of missing things."

"I'm not scared of missing things, I just don't want to. I don't want to miss Heather's wedding. And Abbie's birth-day."

"I come in second?" Abbie asked.

Mom shot her a silencing look. "If anyone understands that, Skylar, it's me. But you can't let fears run your life."

"But leaving home isn't going to solve everything." Ab-bie's gaze pierced me. "Someone really smart once told me that. And she was right."

Mom looked from me to Abbie, then back to me. "Of course it won't *solve* everything. Who said it would?"

"Skylar thinks it will," Abbie said. "She thinks all she needs is a new boyfriend and new friends and she'll be good to go."

"Shut up," I said. "That's not true. I really thought I was supposed to be here. Like if I came to Hawaii, God could . . ." I waved my hands. I didn't know how to say this. "Fix me."

"Fix you?" Dad rested a hand on my shoulder. "What's wrong with you?"

Aaron.

My heart thundered with the thought. Aaron?

I hadn't allowed myself to think about him since that night at Sheridan's, when Jodi told me he and Alexis were together now. I'd briefly worried about her safety and then focused on escaping to Hawaii, where I didn't have anybody like Aaron or Jodi or Connor. Where nobody challenged me because nobody really knew me.

"Hawaii's a wonderful opportunity for you," Mom said. "This'll be the last time in your life when you can just take off. After this, there'll be classes or work or family. I want you to consider staying, Skylar. Think about it, okay?"

I nodded. "Okay."

I sat on the front porch pretending to read a magazine, but really waiting for Justin to get home from work. I wanted him to talk me into staying. Somehow over at the house with the three of them, staying made sense.

Finally, about an hour later than normal, his truck struggled up the road. I made myself wait until he killed the engine, and then I danced across the street.

"Hi," I said with a brilliant smile. "How was work?"

Justin smiled at me, but it seemed bland, as if he felt less than thrilled to see me. "I'd like to talk to you."

"Well, good, because here I am."

Now he didn't smile at all. "But for how long?"

I blinked. "For how long what?"

"For how long are you here? And I want a straight answer this time."

"Okay, what's going on?" I asked. "Why are you acting like this?"

Justin ran a hand through his shaggy hair. "What are you doing with me, Skylar?"

More blinking. What did that even *mean*? "Well, right now I'm standing with you on your driveway feeling really confused—"

"Don't be cute." His eyes, which normally sparkled with friendliness, blazed. "Do you like me?"

"What? Justin, of course I like you. I—"

"I mean, do you like me, or are you just using me to kill some time? To get over someone else?"

I crossed my arms over my chest. "Where's this coming from?"

Justin sighed and ran his hand through his hair again. "Kelli talked to your sister earlier today. I guess she wanted to hold Owen or something, I don't know. Anyway, Abbie told Kelli you're thinking about going home on Thursday with the rest of your family."

I swallowed. "Okay, yeah, I've considered it, but—"

"You said you were praying about staying," Justin said. As if my returning to Kansas City signaled disobedience.

"Would you let me finish a sentence?" I snapped. "I don't know what I'm going to do, okay? I'm trying to sort stuff out. But stop yelling at me. It's not like we were dating—"

"Of course we were! You think I take random girls out to dinner? You think I cook for just anybody?"

I took a deep breath, trying to maintain my cool. "So I

93

guess technically we were dating, since we'd been on dates. What I meant was, I'd always talked about going home in August, and you made it clear you don't do summer flings. I thought we were waiting to see what I decided before we agreed to anything exclusive."

"You're just like my ex," Justin said. "You think you're beautiful and can do whatever you want. You don't care who you hurt."

I could feel my left eye spasm, but of course Justin didn't know to look—something I'd liked so much about him. "That's not fair. Of course I care about hurting you. You're my friend and—"

"We're not *friends*, Skylar. I don't believe in being friends with girls."

I rolled my eyes. "What about Kelli?"

"It's different because she's Chase's girlfriend. Kelli and I don't go out for romantic dinners and then call ourselves 'just friends.'"

"You asked me out," I said. "Should I have said no until I figured out what my life plans were and how you figured into them?"

"If you liked me, it'd be one thing. But I'm beginning to think Kelli's right, that you never liked me. That you were trying to get over someone else and you used me to fill space."

"Kelli said that?"

"She said it Saturday night after you left. I told her she was just being overprotective after what happened with my last girlfriend. I told her you're a nice girl."

I cringed at the description. I wasn't a nice girl, I knew that. And so had sweet, wonderful Kelli. Somehow she'd known my dirty little secret.

"Tell me what Kelli said isn't true," Justin said.

I opened my mouth to say the words but couldn't. "It's true," I said instead. "Kelli's right."

Justin turned and walked away without even saying good-bye.

He left me there to clean up my shattered fantasies about starting fresh, about being a new person here. How could I have been so stupid to think it'd really be that easy? Hadn't I learned by now that the old Skylar still followed me around like a shadow? That she pounced on every opportunity I gave her? And it didn't matter that I'd traveled over three thousand miles from where she'd been created.

The only way I'd ever rid myself of her was to come clean. To open myself up and become so authentic, so light inside, that she had no dark refuge in which to hide.

And to do that, I had to go back.

95

11

"Finally," Abbie whispered as Owen's eyes shut. "I'm never taking him on an airplane again."

"I'm sure he'll get better," I said. "And just think, if he hadn't been screaming his head off, that rude guy wouldn't have been so willing to switch seats with me."

Abbie seemed in no mood for positive thinking. She reclined her seat and continued patting Owen's back. "I'm so exhausted. Who thought taking the red-eye back home was a good idea? Like what I really need is to lose more sleep."

"Then go to sleep."

She gave me a cross look. "I can't just go to sleep. I'll drop him."

"Then give him to me. I'm not tired."

"But you will be in, like, an hour. And then you'll drop him."

"I won't drop him."

She sighed. "No. He's my responsibility. I'll take care of him."

"Stop being cranky and hand him over. If I get too tired, I promise I'll wake you up."

Abbie must have been tired. On a normal day, she'd have gone ten more rounds with me, but she handed over

Owen and curled onto her side as best she could. Instead of closing her eyes, she reached out and stroked Owen's mound of hair. "I'm always hopeful for a break, but then I feel guilty when I get one."

"Well, stop. Just get some sleep."

She sighed and closed her eyes. Despite her awkward positioning, she fell asleep within the minute.

I knew I wouldn't be able to sleep. My mind buzzed with thoughts of returning home. Of everything I'd be facing. Like Connor.

I grimaced. I didn't want to think about Connor. I'd think about Owen instead. His long eyelashes and plump cheeks. The way he sucked his thumb even during sleep. The way he brought out the best and worst in all of us.

Across the aisle, Mom had leaned into Dad's shoulder, and then he'd leaned his head against hers. They both appeared sound asleep, and it brought a smile to my face. How could Grammy not encourage my mom in her marriage? How could she say things like Dad would hurt her again, and use it as an argument for ending the relationship?

Okay, so maybe I'd had kinda similar thoughts about Connor and me, but that was totally different.

Ugh. Okay, it wasn't different at all. It was the exact same lousy reasoning.

I didn't want to forgive him. I didn't want to figure out how to trust him. I wanted to harbor my grudge and find a new guy who'd never even seen Jodi. Was that too much to ask?

I thought of Monday, when Justin and I had dissolved after a mere weekend of a relationship. No matter what he thought, I hadn't *just* been using him. He'd seemed like a nice guy, and I'd liked him. I'd seen possibilities in him. And how quickly his flaws had shown.

But every guy had flaws. It came down to which flaws I could deal with and which I couldn't. Being a super nice guy who wanted to help everyone and sometimes became vulnerable prey for beautiful girls? Maybe that was something I could get over.

I frowned. Of course, I hadn't talked to Connor since he left me those messages about me being over him and moving on and all that. And Lisa had commented on a "vibe" or whatever between him and Jodi. Maybe I was too late.

But I wasn't going back to Kansas for Connor. I was going back for me. For healing. For character.

I turned and looked out the window, at the vast darkness of the Pacific Ocean. Was Grammy really okay with me leaving? Papa had seemed proud, like he thought I'd made the right decision, but Grammy had cried when I told her.

"It's not that I don't want to be here, because I love being with you and Papa. I just don't want to be away from my family right yet," I'd said, in tears myself. I didn't want Grammy reacting like Justin had. I didn't want her calling me out for the horrible person I was.

Grammy patted my hand and put on a smile. "You're a sweet girl," she said. "And we want you to visit as soon as you can."

"Just as soon as Justin moves from across the street," I said, and Grammy laughed and laughed.

My first Saturday afternoon back in Kansas City found me where many others had—standing on Heather's doorstep. I knocked with my elbow since my hands contained cups of Sheridan's custard. Tucked under my arms were bridal magazines and a couple sketches I'd drawn. Knowing Heather, she probably had more ideas than she needed, but the project excited me too much to stifle creativity. It felt good to be productive.

Heather whipped open the door and threw her arms around me. "You're here!"

I hugged back as best I could with the magazines and ice cream.

"Come on in," she said, her blonde hair swishing as she stepped aside.

I stepped into her living room, finding it as I normally did—a chaotic mess of half-folded laundry and various sewing projects. "I can't believe Brent's seen this and still wants to marry you."

Heather laughed, her eyes sparkling. "You should see *his* place. Come on, we're in the kitchen."

We? As in Brent? I blushed at my joke. I'd never have said it in front of him. I barely knew the guy.

I followed her around the corner into her narrow kitchen and stopped in my tracks. Jodi sat at the table, shiny odds and ends scattered before her. It looked like they'd been making jewelry.

"Hey," I said.

Jodi smiled. "Hey. How was Hawaii?"

"Great."

"It's so unfair that a trip to see your grandparents means a Hawaiian vacation," Heather said as she pulled down a water glass for me. "Both my grandparents live in Peoria, Illinois."

"Gotcha beat. Mine are in Wichita and Peculiar, Missouri," Jodi said with a roll of her eyes.

I couldn't stand holding the ice cream any longer and set it on the counter. "Sorry I didn't bring you any, Jodi. I didn't know you'd be here."

"That's fine. I'm trying to lay off. I've gained five pounds since summer started."

I imagined her and Connor seated on the grassy slope at Sheridan's. *Our* grassy slope. I couldn't even find consolation in her gaining weight. The extra pounds seemed to make her prettier.

I looked at the table and saw that they hadn't been making jewelry, they'd been making invitations. "Are these for the wedding?"

"Aren't they cute?" Heather held up one and admired it. "Jodi thought of them."

Of course she did.

"That ribbon's still in my car." Jodi stood. "I'll grab it and get out of your way."

Heather looked crushed. "You're not coming shopping with us?"

"No, I—"

"We need you. Don't we need her, Skylar?"

What else could I say? I cleared my throat. "Sure."

Jodi smiled. "I have to work. Thanks, though." She glanced at me, her dark eyes seeming to search my face. "Skylar, will you help me bring in the ribbon?"

How much ribbon could there possibly be?

With Heather watching, I couldn't exactly call her a lazy bum. "Sure," I said again and trailed after her through Heather's living room.

With the front door secured behind us, Jodi said, "I actually just wanted to talk to you for a minute."

I thought I'd steeled myself for the news of her and Connor getting together, but I suddenly found breathing difficult. And it wasn't just the muggy air.

"I know things have been weird between us for a while now, for lots of reasons. I . . ." Jodi swallowed and looked away. "I don't want it to be like that. I want us to be friends again."

I snorted. The idea of Jodi and me being friends? Flat-out hysterical. I'd been counting down the days until she packed up her car and headed to Vanderbilt. "I really don't see that happening."

Jodi sighed. "I'm not stupid enough to think it'll be easy. We've both done awful things—"

"What have I done?"

"You've dated two of my ex-boyfriends. And one of them you *knew* I still had feelings for."

"You never had feelings for Connor. All he ever was to you was a convenience—"

"That's not true," Jodi said in a sharp voice. Her eyes throbbed with pain. "But I was actually talking about Eli."

"Eli." I blinked a few times. "You guys had been broken up for three years when he and I got together."

"Still." Her voice shook as if she held back tears. "He was my first love, and I wasn't over him. And you'd promised me you wouldn't go there."

"I never would've except—" I clamped my mouth shut before my secret escaped. Only Eli, Connor, and Abbie knew about Aaron. Even Aaron probably didn't know what he'd done. He'd been drinking a lot, and I might just be a blur to him.

His face swam before my eyes—time hadn't dimmed it. His penetrating brown eyes, his square jaw, his mop of dark curls.

"Except what?" Jodi sounded impatient.

"Nothing," I said. "Look, I'm sorry about me and Eli. For lots of reasons. But it's not like I went after him or Connor *while* you were dating. Not like you did to me."

She swallowed. "I know. And I'm so sorry about that. I was a different person back then. That's not me anymore. Surely you of all people can understand that. Our relationship with Christ changes us."

I thought of senior prom, of Connor crushing me by asking Jodi. It'd spurred my second rum-and-Coke night, my second time around with Eli. In the last few months, we'd done more physically than we ever had when we dated, more than I'd even *thought* about before I became a Christian.

And I thought of my last two weeks in Hawaii, the way I'd distracted myself with Justin.

"It's not that simple," I said.

Jodi hadn't been at this as long as me. Soon she'd figure out how the old Jodi still lurked beneath the surface. She'd learn how easy it could be to slip into your old skin. To tell yourself it was okay, that you weren't hurting anyone.

"I better get back inside." I turned away from her, then paused. "But for what it's worth, I'm sorry for what I did."

As we browsed Kaplan's Fabrics, Heather said yet again, "I'm still so bummed that Jodi couldn't join us."

Like I didn't already know this. When Jodi had brought the ribbon inside, Heather begged her once again to come along. Then she bemoaned it at least twice on our short drive to the Plaza.

I kept my mouth shut. It seemed safer.

Heather's hand lingered on a bolt of white silk. "She's such a sweet girl. And she's come so far since this winter. I'm sure you're really proud of her."

So it appeared no one had filled Heather in on Jodi's and my falling out. Well, I sure wasn't going to volunteer.

"Have you decided what kind of white you want?" I asked. "Pure white? Off-white?"

"I'm thinking something more along the lines of this." Heather abandoned the white she'd be so taken with and pulled out a pale, rosy silk.

"You're not wearing white?" How strange. Heather seemed the traditional type of bride. Sure, she wanted something funky for style, but a dress made of shining white suited pure Heather.

"No. Not white." Heather looked at the white silk and said with measured words, "It's not the right choice for me."

And then I knew.

"Oh." I had no idea how to respond. I wanted to say the right thing, something that would let Heather know that it didn't bother me, that I still looked up to her. My head buzzed with about a zillion questions.

"This one's pretty, don't you think?" Heather held the rose against her skin.

"It is," I said, slow and careful. "But I think you should reconsider white."

"I said no white."

She looked desperate for me to drop it. I did.

It was stupid—I knew it was stupid—but I wanted to see Connor.

If he and Jodi really had gotten together, if Lisa had been right about that "vibe" in Starbucks, then I wanted to hear about it from him.

But of course, I had no reason to see Connor. It wasn't like the school days of our breakup, where we shared three classes and lunch, plus rode to and from school together. Most days I'd wished for the summer, for the escape. Now it would have been nice to know there'd be excuses to bump into him, rather than driving to his house and bearing the shame of seeking him out.

After a raging internal debate as I drove away from Heather's, I decided to endure the humiliation.

I second-guessed myself as I dawdled up the walkway. As I punched the doorbell. As I waited for the chaos that normally ensued when someone came to the door at the Rosses' house.

Cevin reached the door first. He yapped and clawed to get out.

What had I been thinking? Clearly jet lag had played a part in this decision. I took a couple steps back. Could I make a break for it? I hadn't even thought out what I'd say to him. Never a good idea with me. I did not do well with improv.

The curtains on the nearest window moved and Curtis's grinning face appeared. "It's Skylar!" His voice came muffled through the glass. "It's Skylar!"

A second face appeared in the window, a little rounder, a little older—Cameron. He gave me his jack-o'-lantern grin. "Skylar!"

Okay, this was nice. Hopefully it'd outweigh the blow of Connor telling me he'd moved on with Jodi.

The two boys rushed out the door and slammed into me, their arms tangling around my waist. Cevin danced around our ankles, yipping as he pranced. Their enthusiasm made my heart soar.

"Hey."

The sight of Connor standing in the doorway—bare feet, swim trunks, and wet hair—dried my throat.

I swallowed. "Hi."

"I heard you were back."

Because he smiled, I tried to do the same. "From Abbie, I assume."

"No." Connor looked uncomfortable. Right. Jodi.

"You'll come to my party, won't ya?" Curtis sashayed around me, his big hazel eyes dancing along with him.

"Of course."

"We're having a pool party." He punctuated this with jumping a couple times. "With Spiderman! And chocolate cake!"

"Sounds sweet." I glanced from him to Connor. Nobody said anything. "Well . . ." I took a couple steps backward. "I just came by to make sure you guys knew I was coming. To the party."

"Can't you play with us?" Cameron asked. "We're gonna play basketball. You can be on my team."

"No, I have to go. But . . ." I glanced at Connor again. "See you guys at the party."

"Wednesday," Connor blurted. His Adam's apple bobbed as he swallowed. "We've got a church softball game on Wednesday. At 6:30. If you want to come."

I nodded, my heart pounding. "Okay."

He seemed surprised. "Okay."

"Okay." I took several more backward steps. "Bye, guys."

"Bye!" the two little ones called after me, but I barely heard them over the pounding in my head.

12

"Do you know if Connor and Jodi are dating?"

Abbie couldn't seem to muster the strength to lift her head off the couch. Instead she rolled her head to look at me, said, "I don't know," then rolled back to the TV. "Why don't you ask him?"

"Because he might say he is."

Abbie snorted. "That sounds like something I'd say. You're normally much more rational."

"I thought you hated that about me."

"Nah." Abbie smiled, but still directed her gaze to the TV. "One of us needs to be."

Owen shifted on her chest and she patted his back until he resettled. His nose whistled every time he breathed. "You don't think I should call the doctor?"

"My experience with infants hasn't changed in the thirty minutes since you last asked me, but Mom said you didn't need to."

She sighed. "If nothing else, I guess he's got his checkup on Wednesday."

The mention of Wednesday brought a rush of heat to my face as I recalled yesterday, the way Connor choked out the word. He wanted me there. He wanted me around. Didn't that mean something?

"What?" Abbie said.

I glanced at her. "What?"

"What's wrong?"

"Nothing."

"Your eye's twitching."

Instinctively I touched the corner of my throbbing left eye. "I didn't know you knew about my eye."

"I didn't." Abbie turned back to the TV. "Connor told me."

"Snitch."

"Have you ever noticed on TV or in movies that characters randomly come and go from rooms?" Abbie asked. "They come in for no apparent reason, say something poignant to our troubled main character, and then walk out for no reason. That never happens in real life. I'm annoyed."

"Want to turn it off?"

"I'm not *that* annoyed. And it's giving me something to think about besides poor Owen." She patted his back. "So what's the verdict? Are you giving Connor another chance?"

I sighed. "I don't know. You think we could ever get past what happened with Jodi?"

"Sure." She didn't give the question the consideration it deserved.

"No, really think about it."

"I don't need to. You love him. He loves you. Why's Jodi an issue at all?"

I frowned at this. I didn't like it being phrased so simply. "He broke up with me for her, yet you want to know why she's an issue?"

"He didn't break up with you—you broke up with him."

"Because he admitted he had feelings for her."

"You practically pushed him into feeling them, Skylar. He was trying to get closer to you, and you kept pushing him away. You expected him to do what Eli did—cheat on you—and you didn't give Connor much of a choice. Same as now. Don't you think if Connor *is* dating Jodi—and I don't know that he is—it's at least partially because he doesn't think you're an option?"

My frown deepened. "But if he's really in love with me, why would he even consider dating her?"

"Maybe he thinks you're telling him to move on. Maybe he thinks you've already started the process. That there's no chance for you two."

I gaped at her. "Did he tell you that?"

"Not so plainly, but I can tell he's thought it." Abbie pinned me with a stare. "If Connor wanted to be with Jodi, he would've started dating her sometime in the last four months. That's gonna have to be enough of an answer for you."

I turned back to the television and so did she, though neither of us really cared about TBS's Sunday night movie.

"Heard anything from Lance since we got back?"

Abbie shook her head. "Jenna said he's got a new girlfriend. Some rich chick who goes to St. Teresa's. Should keep him preoccupied anyway."

"I just can't believe anyone would date him knowing he got a girl pregnant but won't help with the baby."

She shrugged. "I'm sure that's why he's not having much luck with Shawnee Mission girls."

I thought of Alexis's ignorance regarding Aaron. "Guys

like him should be forced to wear a sandwich board or something."

"God knows," Abbie said. "That's enough."

Okay, why did everyone suddenly seem so much more spiritually mature than me? Even my baby sister. Because of course God knew. Of course that was enough. But how come I couldn't internalize that? Why, when I looked at Jodi, could I not think anything but, *Are you for real?*

I should be better about that. I didn't want to be her friend, but I could at least be civil. Unless she and Connor really had gotten together. That'd make it harder.

I sighed. "You know, if you'd told me last summer that I'd be sitting here pining away for Connor Ross of all people, I'd have thought you were deranged."

Abbie grinned. "If you'd told me you'd be pining away for *anyone*, I'd have said the same thing."

"A lot's changed in a year."

Abbie caressed Owen's hair. "And it's not all bad."

Sitting there with my sister, who a year ago had rarely said anything to me outside of, "When are you gonna be done in the bathroom?" I totally agreed.

My first opportunity to be civil to Jodi arrived Wednesday night.

I arrived late at the sports complex because I left the house wearing outfit number seven and hairstyle number four. When I finally spotted our church team (Connor had neglected to tell me which field they'd be playing on), I found Jodi seated in the bleachers with Amy Ross and Cameron and Curtis.

What was Jodi doing here? But her behavior made it pretty clear—she and Amy chatted amicably, their gazes turned toward the field. Jodi looked like a poster child for the perfect girlfriend.

I took a few steps back, but Cameron noticed me before I could flee. "Skylar!"

He and Curtis scrambled down the bleachers. They grabbed hold of my hands to drag me to where they'd been sitting, and when I caught Jodi's eye, victory engulfed me. Quickly followed by shame for feeling victorious.

"Hi, Skylar," Amy said with her normal warm smile. "Sorry I missed you at the house Saturday."

"I didn't stay long." I glanced at Jodi. "Hi."

"Hey," she said, not quite as welcoming as Amy, but much nicer than I'd sounded. "Have a seat."

I took a seat on the other side of her and said a very civil, "Thanks."

Amy filled me in. "We're winning two to one. Connor scored one of the runners, Chris lined out, and Brian hasn't batted yet."

"It sucks that you can't hit them out of the park." Jodi turned to me. "Brian can crank 'em."

Please. Like she needed to educate me on the Ross family.

But, okay, I hadn't known that.

"Mom, we're gonna go play catch," Cameron called over his shoulder as he and Curtis thundered down the steps.

"Stay where I can see you," Amy called after them.

I scanned the baseball field and found Connor in center. Actually, from that distance, I couldn't tell if it was Connor or Chris, but no way would I ask.

"So tell me all about Hawaii," Amy said. "I've always wanted to go."

"It was good. Beach, palm trees. Your basic island stuff."

"Now, I thought you were staying until August. Was that wrong?"

I shifted on my hard seat. "No, I was gonna stay. But I didn't want to be away for that long. With Owen and all."

"I understand," Amy said. "They grow up fast."

"How's Owen doing?" Jodi asked.

"Great. He had his four-month checkup today. He weighs sixteen pounds and is twenty-five-and-a-half inches long. And he had shots. He's in a lousy mood. That's why Abbie didn't come."

Amy cringed. "I hated taking the boys in for shots. How'd Abbie do?"

I thought of my sister in the doctor's office, stroking Owen's head and murmuring, "It's okay. It's okay."

"She did great," I said. "She's able to be really strong for him."

Amy smiled, looking as proud as if Abbie were her own daughter. "She's an awesome kid."

The unmistakable sound of the ball connecting with the bat's sweet spot drew us from our conversation. The ball sailed to the outfield.

"Come on, Connor!" Amy said.

So I'd been right. My heart fluttered as he sprinted after the ball. When he dove for it, my breath caught until he raised his glove, indicating a catch. The three of us whooped and hollered, until Jodi and I glanced at each other and dropped our hands to our laps. Talk about awkward. No way could we ever get past the whole mess of last year.

While the teams switched out, Amy asked, "So did you do anything special in Hawaii?"

"Not really." Justin's image came unbidden. "Laid on the beach. Attempted surfing. Normal stuff."

"I ran into your mom yesterday at the grocery store." She glanced at Cameron and Curtis, still playing catch within view. "She sounded happy to be home."

I smiled, thinking of how many times I'd heard Mom say that since Friday. Before our trip, I'd never heard her speak of Kansas as home, as where she belonged.

"My grandparents' house is pretty small. It was close quarters."

In the dugout, Connor chatted with a teammate. He laughed and shook his head at something the guy said. When he caught me watching, Connor smiled and waved. My heart flipped. I raised my hand to wave back, but then Jodi did the same.

"Oh." I dropped my hand to my lap.

Her mouth formed an O and her face burned red. "Sorry. I'm sure he was waving at you."

"No, I doubt it." My face would've been red too if not for my dark skin. "I don't know why he'd be waving at me, so . . ." I attempted to swallow the lump in my throat. My eyes burned as I battled tears.

"Cameron!" Amy hollered, seeming oblivious to us.

I glanced to where the boys had been playing catch and saw they'd shifted. Only Cameron was visible. When he didn't respond, Amy excused herself and took off down the bleachers, her flip-flops flapping.

Just me and Jodi. Swell.

"So," Jodi said. "We obviously have a problem here."

"Obviously." Though it seemed to me we had a cluster of problems.

"I was trying to tell you something on Saturday at Heather's, but it didn't really come out the way I intended. Actually, it didn't come out at all."

My heart raced. Here it was. Here was where she'd inform me they'd started dating. I formulated my response. "Oh really?" I imagined myself saying. "That's strange, because Connor didn't say anything about it when he asked me to come tonight."

Jodi glanced at me. "It's about Connor, which I guess you pretty much could've guessed."

Down in the dugout, Connor tugged at his collar as he watched us. He knew he should've been the one to break the news to me. Served him right to be anxious.

"I guess it's no secret that I like him." Jodi sighed. "I really didn't want to, but . . ." She smiled at me. "Well, you know how that goes."

AWKWARD.

"I only came tonight because he asked me to." I knew I sounded like a total snot, but I didn't care. So much for civility. "I'm not, like, stuck on him or anything."

"Skylar, it's fine."

"I mean, if you guys like each other, you shouldn't let me get in the way. I certainly didn't let you."

Jodi kinda smiled. "Well, that's true."

"So if you're asking for, like, my approval or whatever . . . you have it."

Shut up, Skylar! This so wasn't what I wanted to say. Though it seemed better than admitting how head over heels I still was for the guy.

Jodi glanced at Amy, who thankfully had started back this way. She could put me out of my misery.

"Look, here's the deal," Jodi said in a rushed voice. "I like Connor. I like him a lot. A week and a half ago, we went for coffee and I told him that. He said he's in love with you." She held eye contact. "I'm getting out of the way, Skylar."

I had no response time since she'd barely gotten her words out before Amy rejoined us. "I'm so sorry about that," she said. "I'm like, 'If you can't see me, then I probably can't see you.'"

I wanted to answer, to be polite, but couldn't. I couldn't do anything but sit there in stunned silence.

Jodi never backed down, especially when it came to guys she felt were rightfully "hers." She'd become a legend for what she did to Sarah Humphrey at a party a couple years ago—she'd heard rumors about Sarah kissing her boyfriend, and when Sarah passed out, Jodi cut off her long, corn-silk ponytail.

So maybe it was true. Maybe Jodi had changed.

13

Jodi didn't hang around after her confession. She mumbled a lame excuse about needing to get home, then rushed out of there. If Amy noticed Jodi's odd behavior, she didn't say anything.

"We've really missed having you around the house," Amy said as the ump called time.

"Yeah, me too."

"We love having Abbie over so much. She keeps us updated on all your goings-on." Amy's face brightened. "Oh! We heard you got all A's your last semester. Congratulations."

Pride swelled in me. "Thanks."

"You worked really hard."

I'd worked harder in school my last semester than the other three and a half combined. I lost a little ground when I split with Connor but still managed to eke out a 4.0. Of course, it only adjusted my overall GPA by a couple points.

"I'm gonna take off," I said, tossing my oversized bag over my shoulder. "I'll see you on Friday for Curtis's party."

"Okay." Amy glanced toward the field, where the players lined up and told each other, "Good game." I thought they just did that in kiddie sports. "Well. I'm sure he—they—appreciate you coming."

"Yeah," I said. "See you later."

I picked my way down the bleachers before Amy attempted to convince me to stay and say hi to Connor. It's not like I didn't *want* to see him, but I didn't know what to say or do when I did. That had my stomach knotted so tight I thought I might throw up.

At the center of the sports complex, where the bathrooms and vending machines were, I heard Connor calling my name.

I turned. He jogged toward me, his cleats sounding hollow against the concrete. My breath caught as I took him in—his large, expressive eyes, his hair curling from the humidity. How could I have disliked him when we first met? How had I missed how special he was?

Connor slowed to a stop a few feet from me. "Hey."

"Hi."

"Why'd you leave without saying bye?" He panted a couple times. "Or hello?"

"I need to get home. Owen had shots this afternoon and is really cranky. I'm sure Abbie's ready for a break." I said it all so fast, it'd be a miracle if he understood half of it. "And I said hello. I waved, remember?"

Connor's ears reddened. Or maybe they'd been that way from playing softball. "Right."

"Good game, though," I said, like an idiot. "Thanks for inviting me."

"Yeah, anytime. We play every Wednesday."

"Okay. Well, maybe I could come next week too."

"Okay."

I shifted my weight from foot to foot. "So, I'll see you at Curtis's party."

"And at church," Connor said. "Although, I guess that's Sunday, isn't it? So I'll see you before. At Curtis's party."

"Right."

His eyes skimmed my face, as if trying to determine what went on behind my mask of a calm exterior. He said something in a rush. I caught "invite" and "Jodi."

"What?" I said.

He took a deep breath. "I said, I didn't invite Jodi tonight. She came on her own."

I swallowed. "You can invite Jodi anywhere you want, Connor."

"Yeah, but I *didn't* invite her tonight. And earlier, I was waving at you."

My heart fluttered. "You don't owe me explanations anymore."

"I *want* to owe you explanations." He blinked rapidly. "If that's okay with you."

"What about Jodi?"

"She's just a friend. She was always just a friend."

"But in the hospital, you said—"

"I know what I said, but my feelings for her weren't like my feelings for you, and I figured that out pretty quickly." He took a tentative step closer. "You were totally right, Skylar. That she was after me, that I had some weird thing about needing to help her. I'm so sorry for what I did to you."

I'd known it already, but hearing it spoken helped to blow out those last flames of anger I'd harbored. I looked around us. "You know what? This is where we met."

"No. We met"—he took several paces toward the men's

bathroom—"here. I could barely get words out of my mouth. You were the most beautiful girl I'd ever seen."

This lured me closer. If nothing else, to keep our conversation as private as possible. Although the other people milling about seemed too preoccupied with their own lives to notice Connor and I having a majorly romantic moment going on. Outside the men's bathroom.

"A lot's changed since then," I said.

His fingers trembled as he reached for me. He tucked my long hair behind my ears and studied my face. "But not everything."

I think he meant he still thought I was beautiful, but I dwelled on the last few months. Of how easily I'd slipped into my old ways. The drinking, the parties. I swallowed—Eli.

"I've kinda had a rough couple months," I said, looking at my sparkly toenails.

He wove his fingers through mine. They fit as perfectly as I remembered. "Yeah, I saw."

My face heated at the memory of him knocking on the Land Rover's door. Of me climbing out of the backseat with Eli.

"I don't know how it happened, really. I never intended to go back to who I'd been. But then . . ." I shook my head. "A cigarette here, a drink or two there, and I somehow slipped back into it."

"That's how it happened," Connor said. "Gradually."

"Maybe . . ." I attempted to pull my fingers free. "Maybe we should wait until I've got my life back in order. Until I've figured some stuff out."

He squeezed tighter, wouldn't let me go. "Or maybe it's

something we can do together. You already know what you want. You know what you're supposed to do. Now it's just doing it."

I looked at him. "You make it sound so easy."

"It's not easy doing it by yourself." He moved closer. I didn't stop him. "I won't let you down again."

"If you did, it'd be okay," I said as his hand rested on my waist, tugged me against him. "I'm stronger now."

He looked in my eyes. "I see that."

I'd never been told anything nicer.

And the kiss wasn't bad either.

The pocket door dividing Abbie's room from our bathroom slid open. "You won't believe who called the house looking for you." She spoke in a normal volume, which meant Owen must have finally settled to sleep in his own room.

"Who?"

"Alexis. And you're lucky I was the one who answered the phone because she was smashed."

I frowned. "Why didn't she call my cell?"

"I think she thought she did. She kept calling me Skylar. I could hardly understand anything else she said. It was super loud behind her."

In my lovesick state, it took me a little bit, but then I remembered Jodi's words at Sheridan's—"You'll never guess who she's been hanging around with. I'm not even sure if you'll remember him. Aaron Robinson?"

I abandoned brushing my hair and turned to Abbie. "You didn't understand *anything* she said?"

She shook her head. "I'm pretty sure she was crying. And she maybe said 'Eli,' but the only thing I heard for sure was your name."

My fingernails bit into my palms. "Was it like an 'I've been abandoned at a party and I need someone to pick me up' kind of call?"

Abbie shrugged.

I returned to my room to find my cell. Abbie followed. "What are you gonna do?"

"Call Alexis, I guess."

"Will you go pick her up?"

My stomach twisted with memories of my one night with Aaron. No way could I abandon Alexis to that. "I don't even know if that's what she needs." My screen glared that I'd missed eleven calls. "Ugh. How long has my ringer been turned off?"

Abbie considered this. "Since Owen's appointment?"

"How is he, by the way?" I asked as I waited for the voice mail lady to prompt me for my password.

"Fine. I gave him some Tylenol. I guess it did the trick." She glanced at my clock—10:30. "I need to wake him up for his last feeding, but I'm nervous."

"About him not going back to sleep?" I asked, but held up my finger to silence her before she could confirm or correct this. Lisa's voice exploded in my ear: "Skylar, you've got to get over to Nick Crawford's, like, right away. Alexis is here with that guy—Adam or what's-his-face from last summer. She's totally wasted and—Madison, that's my beer! No, yours is on the stereo." Hysterical giggling, followed by dead air.

The next message was also from Lisa. She appeared

to have called me by accident, because it was all muffled cackling and bass.

The last message was Eli. At the sound of his voice, I braced myself for hearing he'd beat up Aaron and now needed me to bail him out of jail. "Skylar, you're never going to believe what happened tonight. Call me."

What was with these people? Leave more info!

I punched my speed dial and paced the room while waiting for Eli to answer his cell.

"What'd they say?" Abbie asked.

"Nothing. Three messages and no one said anything even remotely useful."

Then came Eli's chipper, "Hey, girl."

"What happened tonight?" I asked. In the background I heard John's boisterous voice and lots of girly laughter. "Where are you?"

"Sheridan's. You coming out? Lisa said she tried but couldn't get you."

"The ringer on my phone's been off. So what happened at Nick's?"

"You coming out?"

My teeth ground together. "What happened at Nick's?"

"It's better in person. Trust me."

"Well, I just got home and I don't know if I can get back out."

"You should. It's totally worth it. And I haven't seen you since you got back. What's up with that? You avoiding me, girl?"

"She's avoiding me too!" Lisa said in the background.

"Me too!" Madison added.

The entire group's sobriety sounded questionable. Super.

I raked my hands through my hair. "I'm not avoiding anyone. I've been busy."

"You coming, or what?" Eli asked.

I sighed and looked at Abbie. She'd cover for me. "I'll see what I can do."

"What's going on?" Abbie asked when I hung up.

I squeezed my phone in my palm. "I'm headed back to the dark side."

14

I found Eli, John, Lisa, Madison, and several others I didn't know crammed into the bed of John's truck and parked in their normal spot. They were loud and obnoxious, making my head throb with each step closer.

"Skylar!" Lisa squealed as I approached. She clumsily jumped from the truck and ran toward me as best she could in her tall, awkward shoes. Her skinny arms wrapped around my neck—she smelled of sweat and Satsuma.

"Look at you!" She stumbled backward and held me by the shoulders as she assessed me. "Hawaii did you good. Where'd you get that dress? It's so cute." She didn't wait for an answer, just spun and waved at the truckload of people. "Everyone say hi to Skylar!"

"Hi, Skylar!" they chorused.

Eli stood and picked his way around the tangle of legs. He looked good, even though he'd buzzed off his gorgeous blond hair since I'd left.

"Hey, beautiful." He drew me into a too-familiar hug. He always got a little handsy when he'd been drinking.

"So what's going on?" I asked, putting space between us. I noticed several split knuckles. "Oh my gosh, Eli."

"You should've seen him, Skylar," Lisa said. "He was all, 'Do you have any idea what you did to my girlfriend?' and then he just flattened him."

I glared at Eli. "Explain. Now."

"Aww, why you gotta be like that? I knew you'd get all bent out of shape. That's why I wanted you to come down here, because—"

I turned on my heel and stalked toward my car.

"Skylar!" Lisa called after me.

Eli's fingers curled around my wrist when he caught up to me. "Because I knew you'd hang up before I could explain." He held me there beside him, looking down from his six-foot-two-inch frame. "I did it for you."

I pulled away and crossed my arms over my chest. "Walk me through what happened."

Eli sighed and ran his injured hand through his shorn hair. "Well, this afternoon I bumped into Nick Crawford and—"

"Fast-forward to the party. To—" I couldn't say it. "Him."

Laughter rang out from the truck bed as Lisa rejoined the group. Fear struck me. "Do they know? Please tell me you didn't—"

"No one knows anything. But so what if they did, Skylar? You didn't do anything wrong."

It'd been wrong of me to be at the party, to drink so much, to flirt with a stranger, but I didn't split hairs with Eli.

"So he was at the party . . ." I prompted.

"Yeah. I don't know how long they'd been there. Their whole group was pretty loaded, so I'd say awhile. Oh, and you should see Alexis. She looks so trashy. I used to think she was pretty hot, but not anymore."

A lump formed in my throat as I thought of Abbie's account of Alexis—drunk and crying. Not good.

"Did . . ." I forced myself to continue. "Did you see him do the same thing to Alexis that he did to me?"

"I don't think he has to, if you catch my drift." Eli at least had the decency to blush at this. Eli was a good enough guy—he'd tell you so if you asked about his inconsistencies between what he heard Sunday mornings at church and how he acted the remainder of the week. He just liked to have a little fun.

"Anyway, I know you told me to leave him alone, but I saw him standing there and just couldn't help it. I walked up to them and Alexis said, 'What do you want, Eli?' but I ignored her. All I said was, 'Do you have any idea what you did to my girlfriend?' And Aaron said, 'What?' like he was totally confused. Then I punched him. It was a total sucker shot. He fell down, but I think it's 'cause he'd been drinking, not because I'm such a man or anything." He grinned. "Or maybe it was, I don't know."

"What happened then?" I asked.

"What do you think? We hightailed it out of there. He has some big friends. Plus I didn't want to hang around and give the police time to show up."

I suddenly felt too tired to stand and crouched on the cracked asphalt.

Eli sank beside me. "You okay?"

"Yeah, just . . ." My head spun. Why couldn't Aaron have stayed in Florida for the summer? Why'd he have to re-insert himself in my life, a place he'd only briefly been welcome?

"Are you mad at me?" Eli asked. He looked like a little

boy who thought he might be in trouble. I couldn't help smiling.

"No. I'm . . ." I shook my head. "I don't know what I am. I guess Alexis called my house looking for me. I need to try to get ahold of her."

Eli nodded. "You want ice cream or anything? My treat."

I shook my head. No way could I eat.

"Okay. Another time then."

"Do you think Alexis is still at the party?"

Eli shrugged. "Like I said, we got out of there pretty fast."

I moved to stand and Eli helped pull me up. "Sorry if I caused trouble," he said, fingers still tangled in mine. "I just saw that guy and . . . reacted. Thinking about what he almost got away with . . ."

"Thank you for taking care of me that night." I looked up at him through my eyelashes. "You were so nice. And you've been great about keeping all of it private."

Eli shrugged, squeezed my hand. "No big deal. You deserve happiness, Skylar. And now maybe with that jerk Connor out of your life, you can finally have some."

I drew my hand away. "Actually, Connor and I got back together tonight."

Eli blinked rapidly, as if unable to compute what I'd just said. "You *what*? Skylar, what are you thinking? Do I need to remind you what that guy did to you?"

I sighed. "It's really none of your business. And for the record, he never did anything like what you did."

"Yeah, and you've never let me forget it. Do you have any idea how hard I worked all spring to get you back? You just pushed me away. And now you end up with *him*?"

"Don't talk about Connor like that," I said, thinking of all the ways he'd held me together since we met. "You have no idea."

"So, what were you doing with me then? Did these last couple months mean nothing to you?"

I crossed my arms over my chest and looked away. I didn't want to think about things that had happened between us since March. I wanted to close that chapter of my life and be happy with Connor. "You're acting like it meant something to you, and we both know that's not true."

Eli sneered. "How do you figure?"

"Lisa said you've already got some new girlfriend. It seems to me—"

"You left! And you didn't even say good-bye to me. You just got in Connor's car and rode away."

"I—" Like the stuff I'd done with him wasn't bad enough. Knowing I'd hurt him . . . "I'm really sorry."

"Forget it. But I still can't understand what you're doing back with Connor. You know he's just gonna hurt you again."

I bit my lip and forced myself to look at him. "I love him."

Eli rolled his eyes. "Good luck with that."

"That's not fair."

"You expect me to be fair? When I said I loved you, you just stared at me. I'd never said that to anyone before, and you were so . . ." He squeezed his fists, then shook his head and backed away. "Whatever, Skylar. See you around."

"Eli," I said as he walked away, but I didn't follow him. What else was there to say?

He climbed into the truck, smiling as if we'd had a perfectly fine conversation. A cute blonde girl said something to him, and he laughed and threw a friendly arm around her shoulders. He gave me a hard look as if dismissing me.

Alexis didn't answer her cell phone. Instead, my call went straight to voice mail.

I navigated Nick Crawford's curvy, confusing neighborhood, not exactly sure how to get to his house. I'd only been there a few times. Once in eighth grade for a class project and twice in high school for parties.

As the minutes dragged on, my steering wheel grew slick with sweat. What would I be dealing with when I found Alexis? What kind of awful situation would she have to be in before she resorted to calling me? Alexis's problem wasn't with me, but since I hung out with Lisa and Madison, we weren't exactly on speaking terms. Jodi she talked to some, though I'd guess these days they didn't have much in common.

Maybe she'd called Jodi . . .

Before I could think better of it, I held down her speed-dial number. Jodi still held number one, which meant I'd had this phone too long.

"Skylar?" she whispered.

I glanced at the clock—11:15. Not exactly a decent hour to call these days. Used to be she'd have been up for a few more hours at least.

"Sorry to call so late. I wouldn't have, but I had a really weird phone call from Alexis earlier and I wondered—"

"She's sleeping it off on my floor right now. That's why I'm trying to be quiet. Although I'm not sure why." Jodi's voice returned to normal volume. "I could probably go jump on her and she still wouldn't wake up. She's *out*."

"Is she . . ." My stomach twisted as I remembered the nausea of the roofie kicking in. "Does it seem like she just drank too much or . . ."

Jodi sighed. "I guess. When I showed up, she was passed out on the front lawn."

"Where was Aaron?"

"Don't know, don't care."

I'd turned into another cul-de-sac. At least I could stop looking for Nick's house and get out of here. "Well, thanks for taking care of her."

"Yeah. I'll make sure she knows you tried."

"And"—I swallowed—"thanks for earlier. At the baseball park. I think . . ." I so didn't want to say this. "I think Connor and I are giving it another try."

"Okay, good." But Jodi sounded tearful. "I think that's good."

I had no idea what to say, how to fix the tension between us.

An odd sound erupted from Jodi's end of the phone.

"What's that?" I asked.

Jodi giggled. "Alexis snoring. Doesn't she sound just like my dad?"

"Totally. Remember that time I spent the night at your house, and he may as well have been in the room with us, he was so loud?"

"He's using those Breathe Right strips now. I guess they work. He doesn't keep me awake anymore."

"Good." Long pause. "Okay, well. I guess I'll talk to you later."

"Later."

A strange wave of nostalgia hit me as I hung up. It'd been so long since I felt close to someone my age. I needed a friend. A close friend.

15

We'd seen each other three days in a row, but the new-ness still hadn't worn off. When Connor opened the door, dressed for an afternoon of six-year-olds, my stomach did that roller-coaster flip thing.

"Hi," he said, his voice soft and sweet like hot fudge.

"Hi." I stepped inside and made a show of looking around. "Quiet."

"Everyone's out back."

I brushed my fingertips along his pink forehead. "Looks like that's where you've been."

He leaned against me, pressing Curtis's present into my ribs. "Ouch!"

"Oops, sorry." He grinned and took the package from me. "Guess I'm out of practice."

"Me too." I thought of Eli and my face heated. Would Connor remind me of this spring?

He leaned into me, fixing his serious gaze on my face. His lips brushed mine. It'd been like this since Wednesday, both of us a little nervous, a little hesitant. As if we couldn't quite believe this was happening.

A noise startled us. We turned to see a little girl with long, dark braids and dark eyes watching us with an impish grin.

"Hi," Connor said brightly. "What do you need?"

"Bathroom." Her voice rang loud and clear in the tiled entryway.

Connor pointed her down the hallway. "First door."

She turned on her tiny—and pretty stylish for a six-year-old—Mary Janes and flounced down the hall.

I smoothed my hair. "That was embarrassing."

Connor gave me one last kiss before unpinning me from the wall. "It's just Zoe. No big deal."

"Is Zoe somebody I should know?"

Connor whispered in my ear, "Curtis says she steals crayons. I'd watch out."

I giggled and let him lead me through the living room to the sunny backyard occupied by a dozen or so kids. The boys chased each other in a swarm that reminded me of bees, and there appeared to be two gatherings of girls. A few jumped around the moon bounce, and a handful played Marco Polo in the pool. A fluke, or did girls really separate themselves into groups this early? I couldn't remember much about kindergarten except the big timeline my teacher stretched around the classroom so we could count down to the last day of school. The girl sitting next to me had bawled our final day, but I'd sung "Bye!" as I waved and skipped out of the room.

I eyed the moon bounce. "I love those."

"Easy. We got it for the kids. Not people who can legally vote."

"When they leave, we're so getting in that thing."

"Hey, guys," Brian said from the grill. "Great timing. I'm just getting ready to put the dogs on. Or as you kids say it, the dawgzzzz." He made a few weird gestures with his hands, as if throwing around gang signs.

I grinned—Brian's cheesy dad-humor always made me smile—but Connor groaned and tugged me away. "We're gonna go see if Mom needs help. *She's* not embarrassing."

"Oh, she's not?" Brian called after us. "What about all that weeping at your graduation party?"

Sadness pricked my heart. I should've been there. My parents and Abbie had gone, but I'd gone out with Lisa, Madison, and the guys, inwardly crying that none of the Rosses had come to my party earlier in the day. And, not surprisingly, round three with Eli happened that night.

I pushed away those dark, cold thoughts. "She cried at your party?"

"She didn't cry. She *wept*. Dad prayed before they served food, and Mom huffed and heaved all through it."

"Can we put that to rest, please?" Amy said. Her teeth gritted as she pushed on the folding table's stubborn leg.

"Step aside, Mom." Connor brushed her away. "This is man's work."

She winked at me. "We better get Chris then."

"Ha ha," Connor said, followed by a series of grunts as he battled with the table.

Amy shielded her eyes and smiled at me. "I thought Abbie and Owen would be with you."

"She should be here soon. Owen was about twenty minutes from going down for his nap, so she was going to put him down and then come over." I waved my hand, indicating I didn't understand all the details. "I don't know. She worked it all out with Mom and Dad."

Amy sighed. "Good. I was afraid she was avoiding Chris."

"Why?"

My question obviously surprised her—her eyes widened and her mouth opened, though she didn't answer for a moment. "You hadn't heard they broke up?"

"No! When?"

"Yesterday."

"Yesterday?"

I thought back to yesterday, to Abbie. I'd dropped her off at summer school, then Connor and I hung out with Owen. That night we all watched a movie. Connor left twenty or so minutes after Mom and Dad returned from counseling, and then Abbie went to bed just after Owen's 10:30 feeding.

No fits. No tears. No locking herself in her room while she played "their song" over and over. And why not? That would've all been normal Abbie behavior. But this . . . It couldn't get much further away. In fact, it looked like a page from the Skylar Hoyt handbook—I'm acting fine, so surely I feel fine.

"I can't believe she didn't tell me."

I didn't know if I'd said this out loud or in my head until Connor said, "She probably just didn't know how."

"Did you know?"

He righted the table. "Not until I got home last night."

Little boys ran between us, screaming for no apparent reason.

"No running around the pool!" Amy called after them, and Curtis, the leader in his pointy "I'm 6 today!" hat, veered toward the swing set.

"Hey, babe, the grill's ready whenever you are," Brian said to Amy.

"Okay." She turned to Connor and me. "Would you two do me a huge favor? Inside, on the counter, are plates of hot dogs and hamburger patties. Could you bring those out, please?"

As we headed in, Abbie and Chris came out. Abbie looked totally normal. And not like she was trying to look normal, the way you sometimes do when you know you'll see your ex for the first time. She wore regular clothes, a blousy shirt of mine—did I say she could borrow that?—and Bermuda shorts. Her hair hung in a loose ponytail, her makeup looked natural, and her smile looked normal. Not forced. Not heartbroken. Nothing to indicate she stood beside her first love, whom she'd broken up with the day before.

"Oh, hey, guys." Abbie smiled. "What's going on?"

I caught Chris's surprised expression before he masked it. So I wasn't the only one caught off guard by how "okay" Abbie seemed.

"We're getting the food," Connor said.

"We'll help." Abbie turned and trotted off toward the kitchen.

The bounce of her ponytail really freaked me out.

I didn't get a chance to ask Abbie about Chris until we'd eaten lunch, cake had been served, and everyone else was occupied by Curtis ripping into his gifts.

"Amy said you and Chris broke up," I said.

Abbie swallowed a healthy bite of cake. "That's not exactly what happened."

Now *that* made sense. There'd obviously been a misunderstanding. "So, what happened?"

"He flat out dumped me."

I struggled to keep my voice low. "What? How could you not tell me?"

She shrugged. "I didn't know how. I didn't want you to be mad at him."

"Well, too bad." I narrowed my eyes at Chris, who was preoccupied with Curtis.

Abbie gave me a look. "Skylar."

"Walk me through it," I said. "What happened?"

Abbie sighed. "He stopped by school to have lunch with me. I walked him out to his car, or Connor's car, I guess. I said, 'I love you,' and he said, 'I don't think we should see each other anymore.'" She frowned. "Or maybe he said, 'We shouldn't see each other anymore.' I can't remember."

I studied her. "What aren't you telling me? Because I'm not getting it. We're talking about Chris. He's pined for you since the day you met. He calls all the time. He's been nothing but supportive about Owen. So what aren't you telling me?"

"You know everything." Abbie took another large bite of cake. "Look, don't be mad, okay? We always had some idea this might happen."

"*I* didn't."

"Then you're stupid," she said, her voice sharp. "I've got a baby. Not even his father's sticking around."

I hesitated and glanced at Connor. He offered me a tight smile, as if he could guess what our conversation centered on. "Maybe this is one of those self-fulfilling prophesies. Like you expected Chris to fail you, so now he has."

"He didn't 'fail' me. We broke up, that's it. If we'd been able to date from the get-go, it probably would've happened before now." Abbie picked around her last bits of cake. "This doesn't have to be a big deal."

"I just don't understand why you're not more upset. I mean—"

Abbie turned to me, and for the first time I noticed her exhaustion. The normal signs were there—the gray smudges beneath her red-veined eyes—but she had a general droopiness to her. Like Mom's houseplants when she forgot to water them.

"I just don't have time or energy to be upset, Skylar. I've got school. I've got a baby who hasn't gotten the memo that nighttime is sleepy time. I can't indulge in being sad. And even if I could, I—" She drew her vibrating cell phone from her back pocket. "Hello? . . . Yeah, I can hear he is. I'll be right there."

She shoveled in her last bite of cake as she stood. "I guess Owen woke up from his nap two minutes after I left and hasn't stopped crying since. I gotta get home."

I followed her across the backyard. "Here." I handed her my keys. "I can walk."

"You sure you don't mind? Because technically I'm only allowed to drive to school and work."

"It's like two minutes away. I'm not worried."

"Thanks." She slid open the door to the house. "Hopefully in a couple days, I'll have a car of my own and won't have to borrow yours."

I shrugged. "Maybe."

Abbie grinned. "Stop it. Give me a hint. Is it nicer than yours?"

"Actually, they're giving you mine and *I'm* getting a new car."

"Tell them nothing flashy, okay? Nothing red or yellow. Anything black's fine."

"Guess we'll see."

Abbie paused at the front door and glanced back where we'd come from. "Tell everyone sorry."

"I'm sure they'll understand."

She walked backward down the manicured walkway. "You home tonight?"

I shrugged. "I don't know."

"All right. Don't do anything I wouldn't do." At the blind corner, Abbie collided with a guy coming up the walkway. She looked up at him and giggled. "Sorry."

"No problem," he said as Abbie disappeared around the corner with a wave to me.

The sound of his voice made my heart quicken, though I didn't know why until he came closer. I froze in the open doorway. I wanted to yell for Abbie but found myself unable to.

He smiled. A nice, normal smile. If I'd seen him at the mall or something and not known who he was, I'd have smiled back.

"The party still going on?" he asked.

I nodded—amazing I could even manage that.

"Okay if I come in? I'm here to pick up Zoe."

I must have looked at least partially as hostile as I felt because he cocked his head at me. "I'm Aaron Robinson. I'm her uncle."

16

I'd had many dreams—make that nightmares—about coming face-to-face with Aaron. I'd never imagined it taking place at a six-year-old's birthday party. His eye was bruised, presumably from Eli, but otherwise he looked exactly as I remembered.

I stumbled backward a few steps, admitting him into the Rosses' home. My sanctuary.

He sauntered inside. "Sorry, it didn't occur to me that it'd look weird having someone besides Jen picking her up. Guess you gotta be careful about those things these days."

"Everyone's out back," I said, my voice wooden. "They're just about done."

"Cool." Aaron gestured for me to lead the way.

I wanted to sprint outside, to Connor, to anyone safe. I forced my feet to walk at a normal pace.

"Nice place." He gave the huge TV a particular look. "It's your little brother's birthday?"

Tears burned behind my eyes, and I fought to breathe normally. How could he not know me? After what he'd done? After how he'd completely derailed my life?

Connor stood in the threshold of the open glass door.

"There you are." He noticed my escort. "Hey. Who you here for?"

"Zoe."

"I don't know if she's gonna want to leave." Connor grinned—I hated him for it. "She's gotten pretty attached to Curtis's water gun."

Aaron rolled his dark eyes and stepped into the bright sunlight. He didn't belong in the daytime. He belonged in the cover of dark.

It'd been almost exactly a year, but I could still see him in my mind's eye. Plain black T-shirt, tight around his thick arms. His dark curls smelling of expensive gel. Light rinse jeans, frayed at the cuffs. Leather flip-flops.

"You know, I've been watching you the last couple weeks," he'd said, sidling up to me.

I exhaled cigarette smoke. "Oh yeah?" My voice sounded liquid smooth. You'd never have guessed my heart hammered at the sight of the dark, handsome guy talking to me.

"You're friends with those girls, right?" With his red plastic cup he gestured to Alexis and Jodi, who danced on Jodi's couch, their long hair flying.

"Yeah."

"Weird. You seem so much older than them." He sipped at his beer and evaluated me. "There's definitely something different about you."

I shrugged, so flattered it took all my energy to beat back a smile. "Maybe."

"You know what else I've noticed?" He inched closer. "Wherever you are, he is too." He nodded slightly, and I looked. Eli—of course. He stood in the Starrs' kitchen, chatting with a blonde girl anyone could tell he wasn't interested in. He kept looking past her to where I stood.

I shrugged again. "That's a friend of mine."

"Hmm." A few centimeters closer. "So I'm not gonna step on any toes if I get you a drink?"

I shook my head slightly, and he brushed against me. "Be right back," he said.

And I'd hoped he would hurry.

"Skylar," a voice chirped.

I blinked in the bright rays of sunshine. I didn't remember walking outside. I glanced around, head swirling as I fought to grab hold of my bearings. Aaron was nowhere to be seen, which sent a shiver through me. Connor pushed colorful wrapping paper into a large trash bag, and the kids ran wild again.

Cameron danced in front of me. "Hello?"

Beyond him, I spotted Aaron. He stood at the entrance of the moon bounce, talking to an obstructed kid. Zoe, I assumed.

"Skylar! Hello?" Cameron yelped.

Another shiver zipped up my spine as Aaron turned toward us. Recognition dawned on his face, although it didn't seem to bring with it the horror I'd felt at seeing him.

I looked at the little boy hopping in front of me.

"Where's Abbie?" Cameron asked. He bounced from one foot to the other, appearing incapable of standing still.

I couldn't remember. I just stared at him.

"She had to go," someone answered for me, and I turned to find Chris standing behind me.

"Okay." Cameron scurried off, apparently satisfied.

I blinked at Chris, silhouetted by the sun.

His breathing sounded funny. Sharp. "I'm waiting."

"For what?"

"For you to let me have it."

I blinked at him some more. "Have what?"

"Have 'it.' You know. Yell at me."

"Yell at you?" I recognized his breathing now—he did that when he got nervous. "I'm not gonna yell at you."

"Really?" His forehead wrinkled deeply. I'd noticed Amy's doing the same thing when puzzled. "I thought . . ." He shook his head. "I really thought I had it coming."

I had no idea what he was talking about. I opened my mouth to tell him so, but someone tapped my shoulder.

I turned and found myself within inches of Aaron Robinson. He was the opposite of silhouetted—the sun exposed every pore of his face, every swirl of his nasty bruise. I had to give it to Eli, he'd clocked him.

"Now I know where I know you from," he said, grinning. Why would he grin if he actually remembered me? "Didn't we meet at a party last summer?"

"I don't know." My voice sounded hollow, dead.

"Yeah, at that big stone house on Shawnee Mission Parkway. I thought you looked familiar, but I couldn't place you. But how many Skylars are there running around in the world?" He smiled, the same smile that'd haunted me all year.

"You're wrong," I heard myself say. "We've never met."

He seemed amused. "No, we've met. I'm sure of it. I guess I didn't make as big of an impression on you as you did me."

Could he be more wrong?

"You left with another guy." Aaron looked almost sheepish. "I was devastated."

I snorted. "I'm sure you were."

"Well, I just thought I'd say hi. Hey, you seeing anyone now?" He chuckled. Was Aaron Robinson seriously joking around with me? Something new crossed his face, a flicker, and he absently grazed his bruised eye. "Hey, do you know anything about a blond guy who—"

I pointed across the yard to where Zoe—the heinous brat—tortured Curtis with his own water gun. "That kid is like my little brother and your niece is being rude. Please go get her."

I turned away from Aaron's confused face, pushed past Chris, and stormed inside. I didn't slow down until I reached Connor's bedroom. With the door closed behind me, I started shaking. And shaking. My legs could no longer hold me, and I collapsed to the floor. There I shook and shook, reliving every word downstairs.

How dare he not know.

How dare he not be consumed by that night like I'd been.

My fingernails bit into the tender skin of my palms. How was it possible? How could I have suffered so much while he stayed clueless, unaffected?

Laughter reached me, and I crawled to Connor's bedroom window. When I pushed aside the blinds, I saw Aaron and Zoe. He held her hand, and she skipped beside him, giggling. This was my attacker? A guy who picked up his niece from a kid's party?

Could I somehow have been wrong about Aaron? As he helped Zoe into the car, I drew away from the window and sat with my back pressed against the wall. My memories of Jodi's party were fuzzy—especially when it came to what happened after we went upstairs. Maybe I'd been told wrong. Maybe Eli made everything up just to guilt me into dating him. Maybe—

"There you are." I turned to see Connor standing in the doorway, his eyes shining with concern.

"Hey." My voice sounded like a little girl's.

He crossed the room and crouched beside me. "What's going on?"

I shook my head, unable to speak.

Connor misinterpreted. "It's not nothing. Chris said you and that guy . . ." He shrugged. "That there was some kind of history."

"That"—my throat constricted—"was Aaron."

Connor blinked as he processed this. "*That* was Aaron?" His hands raked through his hair. "You were alone with him inside. And . . ." He buried his face in his hands and groaned. "And I just abandoned you out back. Skylar, I'm so sorry." He took my hands between his and squeezed. "I never would've done that if I knew. You should've sent me a signal or something."

"I know, I'm sorry—"

"Don't apologize. No apologizing. If anybody apologizes, it's me. Or him." Connor's face hardened. "Is he still here? I want him out of the house—"

"He left already." I thought of Zoe prancing alongside him as they walked toward the car.

"Good." But his face didn't relax. Neither did his grip.

"Connor, you're squeezing my hands kinda hard."

He eased up. "Sorry. I was fantasizing about the next time I run into him. Boy, I'd like to shake the hand of whoever gave him that black eye."

"Eli."

His eyes widened. "Eli did that? When?"

"A couple nights ago. He ran into Aaron at a party, and . . ." I shrugged. "Well, you saw."

Connor's gaze flicked up and down my face. "Why didn't you tell me?"

"He's not exactly my favorite subject." I picked at the jagged hem of my shirt. I'd been so excited to wear my new outfit, and now it'd been tainted. Same as the clothes I'd worn last July 14. I'd buried them in the garage trash, convinced I could smell the stink of Aaron's cologne in their fibers.

He'd leaned close, his face hovering before mine. "Let's find someplace a little more quiet."

"What just happened?" Connor asked. "You went somewhere else for a second."

"No."

"You did. You were here with me, then your eyes glazed over until I spoke. Is it Aaron?"

I shuddered at his name. "Sometimes I remember things from that night. I can't seem to shut it out completely."

"Maybe you shouldn't."

"I just want it to go away," I whispered.

A gentle knock sounded against Connor's door, then Amy pushed it open. "Hey, guys, this door needs to be completely open when you're up here."

"Sorry, Mom," Connor said.

"Sorry," I echoed. Guilt bit at me, even though it was obvious we hadn't been doing anything. Connor sat across from me. Only our fingers touched.

Amy took a step away, then hesitated. She looked between us. "Is everything okay?"

"Yeah," I said as Connor said, "No."

We looked at each other, then Connor said, "Or at least, we're working on it."

"Okay." She hesitated again. "Holler if you need me."

I sighed as we heard her walk downstairs. "I love your mom."

"You want to talk to her about this?" Connor asked. "I'm sure she'd—"

"No."

"But I bet she'd—"

"No."

Now he sighed. "Okay. What about me?"

"What do you mean?"

"I mean, how about talking to me about it?"

I squirmed. "No."

"Why not?"

"It's just . . ." I looked at him, wonderful, innocent Connor. I didn't want to shed any more light on who I used to be. I wanted to close the book on her and move on. Why couldn't I? Why should I be forced to remember everything? Maybe there was a reason I couldn't. Maybe I wasn't supposed to remember.

I looked at our entwined fingers rather than his face. "I don't want to dredge up everything. I don't want to be forced back there."

"But maybe"—he touched my fingers to his mouth—"it's the only way you'll be free to move forward."

17

"Surprise!" Dad whipped the blindfold off Abbie.

She stood there staring, her face frozen in a smile. "Wow. Thank you." But both her voice and her smile wobbled.

I caught Mom and Dad glancing at each other over her head.

"It's got everything," Dad said, now doing the hard sell. "Leather interior, navigation system, speakers so good you'll lose your hearing by the time you're my age."

"It's great," Abbie said as fat tears squeezed from the corners of her eyes. "And it's so . . . shiny."

I looked at the car. Dad hadn't skimped a penny. This baby was tricked out. As tricked out as any silver Toyota Camry sedan could be. Complete with an installed car seat.

"I don't mean to be crying," Abbie said, wiping away tears. "I'm not even sure why I am."

I gave the car another glance. I could venture a guess.

"Here you guys did this incredibly nice thing for me, bought me a beautiful, expensive present, and . . ." Abbie said more, but her tears strangled her words beyond recognition. When Mom offered her arms, Abbie fell into them, sobbing.

"It's okay," Mom said. She shot Dad a look, as if this whole mess was his fault. Dad frowned at the car, clearly unsure about where he'd gone wrong. I patted his shoulder with my free hand—Owen occupied the other—but he didn't seem to notice.

"It's stupid," Abbie said. "After what I did, I don't even deserve a birthday gift, and—"

"Nonsense," Mom said, her mouth a firm line.

Abbie sniffled. "It's a perfectly good car."

"Perfectly good?" Dad said. "She's brand new. She's beautiful. I don't understand what the problem is." He watched the two of them, waiting for an answer. "Well?"

"Not now, Paul," Mom said.

"Want to know what kind of car I got for my sixteenth birthday?" he said. "I didn't. I didn't get my first car until I left for college, and that's because I worked whenever I wasn't at school and saved every blasted dime—"

"Enough," Mom snapped as Abbie started up again.

"He's right," Abbie sobbed. "He's right. I'm ungrateful."

I smoothed Owen's hair and watched him blink at his bawling mother.

"He didn't mean it like it sounded," Mom said in an attempt to soothe Abbie.

"I didn't mean it?" Dad sounded even more irritated. "Don't tell my daughter what I did or did not mean."

Mom shot him a look, a "shut up" kind of look.

My parents, the great communicators.

I cleared my throat. "I think what's going on"—they turned to me—"is Abbie's just trying to deal with not having a . . . normal car."

"A normal car?" Dad said. "What's more normal than

a Toyota Camry? I see these things on the road all the time."

"Being driven by a sixteen-year-old?"

Dad blinked. "Well, no." And then it seemed to dawn on him. He turned to his weeping daughter. "Abbie, I assumed you'd prefer something like this. A two-door car with a baby is no fun. That's what we had when Skylar was born, and . . . Well, I wasn't thinking about how you might feel about a sedan."

No surprise. The psyche of high school girls wasn't exactly my father's expertise. When Abbie and I were little, he'd get down on the floor and wrestle with us. He'd let us style his hair and then drink "tea" with our dolls. But around the time I started needing Tampax, he stopped knowing how to interact with me.

"You're right." Abbie wiped at her face, smearing her mascara. She'd been all made up and ready to hop in her new car and head to school. "You're absolutely right. I need four doors, and Toyotas are great cars. It's fine. It's great."

Dad hesitated. "We can go look at other cars. Or other colors—"

Abbie shook her head. "This makes the most sense. It's just me . . . adjusting, I guess." She took Owen from me and hugged him close. "Not that I'd give him up, but . . ."

"I know." Mom draped her arms around Abbie and Owen. "Trust me, I know."

It set off a strange mix of emotions inside me, watching as they bonded over an unexpected birth. As if Owen and I had plotted to come along early and ruin their lives. But I suppressed my hurt feelings. After all, Abbie didn't need me sulking on her sixteenth birthday. Like the day

wouldn't be tough enough. A rocky night with Owen, summer school, no boyfriend, and a brand-new car that may
as well have been a minivan. Not even a birthday party to
look forward to.

"I should go," Abbie said with a heavy sigh. She returned
Owen to me, but he didn't seem to notice. Abbie frowned.
"I know I gripe on the days he wants only me, but some-
times it'd be nice if he cried just a little bit."

"Don't wish evil on your babysitters," I said.

Abbie wrapped her bare arms around Dad's neck. "Thank
you, Daddy."

His face creased with a frown my sister couldn't see.
"Happy birthday, little girl."

We stood there and watched as she adjusted the seat,
turned the ignition in her new car, and backed down the
drive. She grinned and waved before putting the Camry
in drive and heading for school.

"You should've gotten her a Jeep or something," Mom
said as Abbie turned off our street. "Something with four
doors, but still sporty."

Dad sighed. "She'll adjust. It just wasn't what she expected."

"But when you buy an expensive gift like that, you want
them to like it."

"Then maybe there's something wrong with our parenting," Dad said, "that we raised a kid who wouldn't appreciate
a brand-new car."

Mom gaped at him. Clearly that hadn't been the right
response.

Before they could get into it, I turned and carried Owen
back into the house. I cuddled him close to me, still unable

to shake the feeling that I'd been unwanted, a disappointment. "Not you, pal." I pressed my cheek against his. "We want you."

About a week ago, Mom had invited the Ross family to join us for Abbie's birthday dinner. It'd seemed like a harmless idea, something to make Abbie feel special since all her stupid, catty friends had abandoned her. They'd been strangely excited about Owen before he arrived, had enjoyed buying him adorable yet impractical clothes. They visited in the hospital and took turns holding him, but now that the reality of his existence kept Abbie from being much of a sixteen-year-old girl, even the most faithful of her friends had fallen away. And I couldn't believe I could now add Chris to that list.

Maybe it was stupid to think a couple of fifteen-year-olds could make it, but I always thought Abbie and Chris would. I mean, somebody from high school has to, right? Like Brian and Amy Ross. And the idea of Chris breaking up with my sister . . . I still couldn't wrap my mind around it.

"Is there something you'd like to tell me?" Connor murmured in my ear as we ate.

I turned. "What?"

"You've been staring at Chris all night." He grinned. "I'm getting a little jealous."

"Sorry. I didn't realize it." I pushed my baby carrots around on my plate. Since running into Aaron on Friday, I hadn't had much of an appetite. Go figure.

Chris glanced at me and shifted in his seat. He murmured

something to Abbie, who shrugged. How could they act so normal around each other? After our breakup, Connor and I had never felt comfortable around each other.

"Skylar, any updates on your college plans?" Amy asked as she dished herself more mashed potatoes. "You're not still thinking nursing, are you?"

Abbie snickered. "Yeah, she'd be a real comfort to her patients."

Last winter, I'd briefly entertained the idea of becoming a nurse. I'd even declared it my major at Johnson County Community College. But my dreams of a noble profession died when Owen came along. When the anesthesiologist had given Abbie her epidural, I'd fainted. It left a nasty bruise on my forehead and my pride.

"I've given up that idea." I shrugged. "I don't know what I want to do."

Everyone but Cameron and Curtis stared at me. Obviously, I'd said something wrong.

"What?" I said.

Mom sighed and looked at Amy. "See what I mean?"

Amy just smiled.

"Hello?" I said. "What's going on?"

No one answered. Finally, Mom took a deep breath. "I think we're all just confused about why you're not pursuing what you love and excel at. Fashion. Design."

I poked at my carrots some more. "Let's not go there."

"I agree," Abbie said with a cheeky grin. "Tonight's about me. We talk about Skylar enough the other 364 days of the year."

When everyone else laughed, I forced a smile. I appreciated the diversion, but what was with Abbie these days?

She had a snarky comment for every ounce of attention I received. Like she didn't get enough being sixteen and having a baby.

We finished dinner without me having to say another word. As the parents cleaned up dishes, Cameron and Curtis rushed out back. When Connor, Chris, Abbie, and I joined them a few minutes later, they'd engrossed themselves in some game with discarded pinecones from our evergreens.

Abbie relaxed in one of the teak chaise lounges, her auburn hair fanning out behind her. She closed her eyes and didn't see what I did—the hungry way Chris looked at her. It lasted only a few seconds. By the time Abbie cracked open an eye, Chris had turned toward his little brothers.

"Skylar, did you grab the monitor?" Abbie asked.

"No."

"Do you mind?"

"Mom and Dad are inside. I'm sure they'll let us know if Owen's crying."

Abbie sighed. "I'll go get it."

"No, stay there." I stood from the seat I'd just cozied into.

"Thanks!" she called after me.

I repeated to myself that this was a hard day for Abbie. That my sixteenth birthday party had been worthy of an MTV episode. My new car had been an ebony Acura RSX. I'd spent my morning sleeping and my afternoon loafing around the country club pool. I'd flirted with random guys and let Eli kiss me because I liked the idea of getting my first kiss the day I turned sixteen. He'd looked so happy when he leaned close and I didn't push him away. And then he'd whispered in my ear . . .

My mind flitted back to the party a year ago, to Eli finding me in the Starrs' guest bedroom.

"You're okay." Eli's arms had circled my torso, lifted and pulled me close. My shirt rode up, but I couldn't finagle it back down. When I'd bought it a couple weeks back, I wondered if it'd be a problem, but I assumed I'd always be capable of adjusting it. I hadn't anticipated this. Whatever this was.

"What's going on?" My tongue felt heavy and foreign in my mouth—how was that possible?

"You're okay," Eli repeated. "I've got you."

"Skylar?" Connor's voice reached me.

I blinked, finding myself not in the guest bedroom of the Starrs' house, but on my back porch, one hand resting on the doorknob.

I turned and found the three of them watching me. "What?"

Connor stood. "You okay?"

I nodded and pushed the corners of my mouth into a smile. "Yeah. Just . . ." I shook my head. "Zoned out for a second."

He looked like he didn't buy it, like he knew I'd gone to my "other place." But if I admitted that, he'd push even harder for me to open up about that night. The isolated moments I recalled seemed horrible enough. I feared what I'd discover if I pieced them together.

18

Heather beamed as she held up the pinned bodice of her wedding dress. "What do you think?"

"It's awesome." I couldn't help reaching for it, feeling the slippery silk between my fingers. "You're going to look amazing."

"Why can't it be August 1 yet?"

"We're close."

"Three weeks and two days."

I grinned. "See?"

"Last night, I did the seating arrangements for the reception. I loved placing you and Connor beside each other." Heather fit the bodice onto her sewing machine. "How's everything going?"

"Great." I smoothed Heather's veil on my lap. "It's like when we first started going out. Before . . ." Heather still didn't know about Jodi. "Before things got complicated."

Heather's brow creased. "Complicated how?"

"You know. Just how things tend to get complicated sometimes."

She leaned forward in her chair, wedding dress temporarily forgotten. "Complicated how?" she repeated, slower, more serious.

I took a breath but just looked at her. If I told her about Jodi, she'd see what a horrible Christian I'd been. That I hadn't wanted Jodi at church or youth group, that I'd been hostile toward her and did nothing to encourage her transformation. I'd made it all about me and Connor.

"Did you and Connor have sex?" Heather asked.

"What? No!"

She burst into laughter. "Oh my gosh, what a relief. You kept using the word *complicated* and you clearly didn't want to tell me what'd happened . . ."

"I can't believe you thought we'd do that. Never. Never ever."

Heather shrugged. "I'm glad you feel that way, but sadly it's not always that cut-and-dried. You're eighteen, you're with the guy who you think could be 'the guy' . . . All those lines can get kinda fuzzy."

"My lines aren't fuzzy."

"Good." Heather assumed a sewing position but didn't press her foot to the pedal. Something about the look on her face reminded me of a couple weeks ago, at Kaplan's, when I'd been 99 percent sure she'd already lost her virginity.

"But I know what you mean," I said. "It's easy to get fuzzy."

The sadness in her eyes made me ache. "You've no idea."

I bit my lip and focused on sewing beads to the trim of Heather's veil. "Do you want to talk to me about something?"

She sighed. "It was a long time ago."

"Doesn't mean we shouldn't talk about it."

A long silence ensued. I peeked and found Heather staring at the bodice of her rosy dress.

"There was a guy," she said, her voice clear and calm. "We'll call him . . . Guy. Guy and I met in high school, at youth group, actually. He was amazing. Good-looking, funny, intelligent. And so passionate about the Bible. I thought he was it."

Her mouth quirked into a strange smile. "I had these fantasies about getting married and spending our evenings drinking coffee and having great theological discussions. He wanted to be a pastor, and I was going to be the perfect pastor's wife." Heather rolled her eyes at the memory of herself. "I was such a dork, Skylar. I asked for a mixer that year for Christmas because I wanted to learn how to bake the best cookies."

"You weren't a dork," I said.

"That's when I learned how to sew too. My mom didn't know how, so I begged Grandma to teach me. It was all about him, Guy. It was always all about Guy."

"So what happened?"

"It wasn't as dramatic as you might think," Heather said, fretting with a pin. "We used to go to this parking lot after dark. Sometimes we just talked. A lot of times we fooled around. This went on for a couple years, and then one night . . ." She shook her head. "We let it go too far.

"Neither of us knew what to do on the drive home. We just sat there in the car like stones. And when we pulled into the driveway of my parents' house, Guy said, 'Maybe we should take a break.' You'd think it'd have devastated me, but I felt so relieved. 'Yeah, we should,' I said. And that was basically the end of it."

"That was the end of it?" I said. "A break?"

Heather nodded. "We saw each other at church, of course. But then he left for Bible college and I stuck around here for school. My parents are still friends with his parents. I hear stuff about him sometimes. He's a pastor in Rhode Island and has twin girls." She shrugged, as if this were no big deal.

"Do you still love him?"

Heather frowned. "I've thought about that a lot, about if I ever *did* love him. Have you ever read *The Great Divorce* by C. S. Lewis?"

I shook my head.

"Okay, then never mind, because I can't explain it like he does."

"Try."

"Well, he's got this theory that when you're in heaven and looking back on your life, you'll feel that everything was for good. Even those really sucky times, you'll see how it all pointed heavenward. On the other side, if you're in hell looking back on your life, you'll feel everything was for bad. That you were always in hell. Make sense?"

I hadn't thought so hard since I took my last final. "Kinda."

"Okay. Well, I think it's like that with me and Guy. If it'd all worked out and it was *me* with him in Rhode Island with twin girls, I'd probably think I truly loved him in high school. But now, feeling what I do for Brent, what I had with Guy doesn't seem like love at all. It seems like . . . nothing."

I stared at the shopping bag full of "whisper pink" tulle. "And this is why you won't wear white at your wedding? Because of one night in high school?"

Heather blinked at me. "A white dress symbolizes purity. Other women disregard it. I refuse to."

"But what about forgiveness?" I bent my head, focused once again on the beading. I didn't want Heather seeing how my eyes had pooled. "Some of us have done a lot worse stuff than you. You've always told me I'm forgiven, so why doesn't that apply to you?"

Heather paused. "I guess it's like with Abbie. She's forgiven for having sex outside of marriage, but God didn't take away Owen. There's still cause and effect."

"I think that's an excuse," I said. "I think everyone has forgiven you except you. And you should wear a white dress."

I couldn't say what I wanted to most—that I *needed* her to wear a white dress. I needed her to teach me to forgive myself.

Heather's mouth pressed into a firm line. "I have to get ready for work." She left the room, leaving no question in my mind that the time for me to leave had come.

I let myself out the door without saying good-bye.

When I entered my house through the garage door, it was clear Mom and Dad hadn't heard me arrive.

"That's not what this is about," Mom said. It sounded like they stood in the kitchen. "Why do all our arguments turn into you concluding that?"

"I think it's a valid point."

"It's *not* a valid point. Especially because I'm telling you that's not my issue with you working late."

"And I hear what you're saying, but—" Dad spotted me and put on a smile. "Oh, hi, honey. How was Heather's?"

"Fine."

Mom turned, her smile forced as well. "You make much progress on the dress?"

"Some."

Then we all just stood there.

"Well, I'm gonna go upstairs." I turned and left them to finish their argument in privacy.

That gnawing feeling had returned, that my parents couldn't make it work. That the path they'd started on last fall, when Mom left and started pursuing divorce, would eventually manifest itself.

I didn't doubt Mom and Dad wanted to reconcile. They'd been going to counseling and seemed to be controlling each of their vices pretty well—Dad's hours at the office and Mom's overspending. But I continued to feel as though the other shoe would soon drop. That once again Mom would split, Dad would pretend it was normal, and Abbie would close herself off. Once again I'd be left to piece the Hoyt family back together.

As I entered the hallway, I heard crying. Not Owen's scratchy cry, but Abbie's heart-wrenching sobs.

I crept into our bathroom and peeked through the gap between the door and the wall. Abbie knelt beside her bed, beautiful red hair streaming into her face, blocking my view. Her narrow frame shook, and she looked so much like a child. How had she possibly given birth just a few months ago? In the corner of her room, Owen snoozed in his bouncy seat, blissfully ignorant of his mother's emotional state.

"Please, God, help me," Abbie choked out. "I don't know how to get over Chris. I don't know how to balance school.

I don't know how to do anything. I'd swear you said you wanted me to raise Owen. Please show me how. Please make me stronger. Make me better."

I backed away from the door, restoring Abbie's privacy. She didn't need me. She was in good hands.

19

"That's the ugliest thing I've ever seen."

I smiled at Connor, who'd materialized behind me. "I didn't hear you come in."

"What *is* that?" Connor leaned over my shoulder to look at the screen of my laptop.

"It's freaking awesome, is what it is," I said, turning back to the picture of a Claire McCardell pattern. "Think I could pull it off?"

"Why would you want to?"

I frowned. "Easy, okay? Be nice to Claire."

"What's with the bow on the butt?"

"I wouldn't make it with the bow. Or not one that full, anyway." I enlarged the image. "I don't know what kind of fabric she intended. I was thinking polished cotton. Wouldn't it be perfect for Heather's wedding?"

"I don't know." He squinted at the photo. "What year's she getting married in?"

I grinned. "Hopefully 1957."

"You're gonna look like one of those old-timey house-wives."

"I won't. You'll see." I clicked to add the pattern to my shopping cart. "Just a sec and I'll be ready to go."

"Take your time." He stretched out on my floor. "Your carpet smells nice. Mine smells like dog."

"Cevin's a nice-smelling dog, though."

"Not this morning. He got in the garbage. Mom was livid."

I smiled as I typed in my credit card info. "I can't imagine that."

"It happens." His stomach growled. "I know I said to take your time, but—"

"Thirty more seconds."

"You and Heather make up yet?"

I hadn't told Connor what Heather and I fought about yesterday, just that we had. "Not yet. Hopefully by her bridal shower."

"When's that?"

"Next Saturday."

"Tomorrow?"

"No, *next* Saturday." I closed the lid of my laptop. "If I'd meant tomorrow, I'd have said tomorrow."

"But tomorrow is the next Saturday."

I sighed. "Wanna go to dinner by yourself?"

"You know you don't mean that." He stretched up his hand, and I tugged him off the floor.

"Oof," I said as he stumbled into me. "Graceful."

"Why, thank you." His hands pressed into the angles of my hipbones as he steadied himself. Our gazes met, and I had one of those moments. I knew I was a girl, he was a boy, and we were standing in an empty house.

"Don't take this the wrong way," he said, "but we should leave."

I smiled. "You read my mind."

After a swift kiss, Connor took my hand and we headed out the door.

"So I need you to answer something for me," Connor said as we perused the dinner options at Houlihan's.

"Hmm?"

"Why are you struggling so much with what to major in?"

I bristled. He knew how much I hated this topic. "Lots of people struggle with what to major in. *You* don't know."

"That's because I've got no obvious talents."

"Are you kidding me? You're so artistic! That sketch you made of—"

He halted me by holding up a hand. "I don't want to debate that. I want to talk about why you're not pursuing design, or fashion, or whatever you want to call it."

"Don't even want to wait until we place our order, huh?"

He smiled. "It's not that hard of a question. Come on, now. Straight answer."

"Straight answer?" I shrugged. "It just doesn't seem like the right thing to do with my life, you know? I mean—fashion. How pointless is that?"

"I think you're looking at this all wrong," Connor said, leaning forward. "It's not that—"

"Hey, guys."

I looked up to find Eli towering over us, his arm around the same cute blonde girl I'd seen in the truck.

"Hi," I said.

"You guys know Marin?"

We shook our heads.

"This is Marin. Marin, Connor and Skylar."

She barely glanced at Connor, just zeroed in on me. Her eyes narrowed slightly with her assessment.

"Hi," I said.

"Hey," she said, her word a mere wisp.

The waiter appeared with Connor's and my drinks. He glanced at Eli and Marin. "What can I get you two?"

I opened my mouth to explain they weren't with us.

Eli slid into my side of the booth. "I'll have a Coke. What about you, Marin?"

I turned round eyes to Connor—had our date just been hijacked?

"Water," Marin said. She perched on the booth next to Connor, looking totally uncomfortable. All of us did except Eli and the waiter.

He placed the drinks on the table. "Be right back."

"Dr Pepper?" Eli asked, winking at me.

"Uh, yeah."

"That's our girl, huh?" Eli said to Connor, his smile big and fake. He stretched his arms along the back of the booth. He didn't touch me, but still. Weird.

"Could you move your arm, please?"

"Right. Sorry." He flashed Connor another smile. Dimples, crinkled eyes, the whole charming package. "Haven't seen you for a while, man. What you been up to? Besides stealing my girl, that is. For the second time." He punctuated this with a big, hollow laugh.

A twentysomething couple at a nearby table glanced our way. I wanted to crawl under the table and slither out of the restaurant.

"I'm not even sure I should let Marin sit over there with you," Eli said. "I might leave the restaurant with no one."

Connor took a deep breath but didn't say anything, just looked at me. He seemed as dumbfounded as I was.

"Maybe you two should sit at another table," I said.

Eli turned to me, his eyes round. "Why?" He said it big and breathy. I hoped to smell alcohol—an explanation—but didn't.

"This is really awkward." I glanced at Connor and Marin. "I think everyone would be more comfortable if—"

"If we just didn't talk about what's going on?" Eli said. "That's your philosophy for everything, isn't it, Skylar? Don't talk about it. Don't tell anyone."

"Look, man—"

Eli shot Connor a look that shut him up. "Don't even start with me. Has Skylar told you what it was like with her and me this spring?"

The twentysomething couple looked our way again.

"If you're going to keep talking, will you at least lower your voice?" I asked.

"Eli, let's go to another table," Marin said. Her face bloomed crimson. She was probably very nice, and Eli was blowing it with her over some stupid vendetta.

Eli ignored her. "You could've called me from Hawaii, you know." His blue eyes accused me. "But you just got out of the Land Rover and left. With *him*."

"Look, I'm sorry I didn't say good-bye. That was a rotten thing to do. But—"

"But you don't care about me. Right?" Eli smirked. "Just like you've never cared about me. Not this spring. Not when we were dating. And not last summer when you'd been flirting with me all day at the pool, only to go to Jodi's party, where you practically threw yourself at that preppy—"

"That's enough." I looked across the table and saw that Marin had been smart enough to leave during Eli's tirade. "If you're not gonna go, we will."

I thought Eli would put up a fuss, but he slid out of the booth. "Fine. Go. But you know next time Connor screws up and starts kissing girls who aren't his girlfriend, I'm not gonna be around for you to rebound with."

"I can only hope," I said as I stood. Connor stalled my triumphant march out of there by throwing down cash for our untouched drinks. So not the time for his conscience. But it gave me time to say, "You used to be a real nice guy, Eli."

He swallowed. "I'm a sore loser."

How sore?

"Best of luck, Connor," Eli called after us, his voice jovial. "She gets bored easy."

"I didn't throw myself."

Connor glanced at me. "What?"

We'd been silent since we left the restaurant, both of us isolated in our own minds. I hated to consider what he might be thinking.

"Eli said I was throwing myself at Aaron that night. I wasn't."

Connor nodded, appearing to ponder this. "How do you know?"

If he'd said it to tick me off, it worked. "How do I know?" I demanded. "Because it's not something I do. Ever."

He shrugged. "You were drinking a lot. You'd possibly been drugged. How do you know how you acted?"

"Is this your way of comforting me? Because I gotta tell you—it stinks."

We'd stopped at a red light, and Connor turned to me. "Do you need comforting?"

"My ex-boyfriend just made a scene at a decently nice restaurant. I could use a little comforting. And the light's green."

Connor punched the accelerator and the SUV jumped forward. "You handled yourself so well in there. I didn't think you needed to be comforted."

I crossed my arms over my chest. I needed Connor to tell me that what he'd witnessed back at Houlihan's, the stuff he'd heard Eli say, hadn't changed his mind about me. That he still wanted us to be together.

Unfortunately, he couldn't read my mind and remained silent.

"Where are you going?" I asked as Connor turned into a random parking garage.

"We need to talk."

"In *here*? It's creepy."

"Well, where do you want to go?"

"I don't know. What do you want to talk about?"

He gave me a semi-exasperated look. "I want to talk about that night."

"I don't want to talk about it! I've told you that, like, a thousand times!"

"I think you need to," Connor said, keeping his voice steady even though I'd screeched.

"Why?"

169

"Because I'm wondering if Eli told you the truth about what happened or if he's making it up."

"Making it up? What would he be making up? *Why* would he make something up?"

"Were you at the same table as me tonight?" Connor asked. "He said it right to your face—he's a sore loser. And the night of Jodi's party, it sounds like he thought he lost."

"I wasn't his to lose."

"I don't think he saw it that way."

I swallowed and turned my back to him. Eli had been right—I'd been flirting with him that day. In four days, it would be exactly a year since the day of Jodi's party. We'd been at the pool, baking in the sun. I'd leaned too close to Eli when I talked, brushed against him whenever I could. It sickened me to think of it now, my silly mind games. What would Connor think if he knew? Good-bye, happy, healthy relationship.

"I don't want to talk about this," I said. "I don't know how else to say that to you."

"I know you don't, and I get it, but your entire truth of that night is based on stuff Eli told you. And after what I just witnessed, I don't know if he's the most credible source."

"Don't say that." I couldn't believe how menacing my voice sounded. "I know he's not your favorite guy in the world—he's not mine either—but he rescued me that night."

"Here's what I can't figure out—"

"What part of 'I don't want to talk about it' do you not get?"

"—if he saw Aaron put something in your drink, why

didn't he do something right away? Why wait until you were already up in the bedroom?"

I remembered Eli lifting me off the bed like I weighed nothing, his voice warm in my ear as he told me I'd be okay. And I had been, because he carried me out of there and kept me safe.

"Take me home," I said in a flat voice. "I have nothing else to say to you."

20

When my stomach growled a couple hours later, I realized I'd never actually eaten dinner that night.

"I'm starving," I said to Abbie. "You want anything?"

Her eyes never left the Lifetime Original Movie. "Nah."

As I dished myself leftover Pad Thai, Abbie called to me, "I thought you and Connor went to dinner."

"We didn't stay. Eli was there."

"Is that what you fought about?"

I hesitated. "Who said we fought about anything?"

She snorted. "Please. You stormed through the door hours before curfew with your face all scrunchy. How stupid do you think I am?"

I didn't answer, just stared at my plate of food spinning in the microwave.

When I turned around, Abbie stood in the kitchen as well. She opened the freezer.

"I thought you weren't hungry," I said.

"I'm not." She pulled out a half gallon of mint chocolate chip. "But it's the first Friday night I've got my driver's license, and I'm at home." She grabbed a spoon. "I'm eating till I hit cardboard."

"Go for it."

We both padded back into the living room, where Mom forbade us to eat. We did it anyway when she was out. Tonight she and Dad had gone to a black-tie fund-raiser of some kind. Or maybe that was tomorrow night and tonight they'd gone to a movie. I couldn't keep track.

"How lame is it that our parents have more of a social life than us?" I said.

"Totally." Abbie sighed. "You could, though. At least you've got a boyfriend."

I thought of how I'd seen Abbie yesterday, crouched beside her bed, begging God to help her get over Chris.

"You want to talk about Chris yet?" I asked.

She seemed surprised by the question. "Is there something to talk about?"

I shrugged. "We haven't discussed it much. I just thought you might want to."

"Nope."

"O-kay."

Abbie rolled her big, cinnamon eyes. "Don't do that."

"What?"

"Say 'okay' like that. Like you think I'm holding out on you."

"You're not?"

"No."

"Abbie. You told Chris you loved him and he broke up with you. But you don't want to talk?"

"No."

"You're not upset?"

She laughed. "Like I said, I was really just surprised it didn't happen sooner. Guys like Chris don't date girls like me."

173

Her words wounded me. As if girls like us didn't stand a chance with nice guys. "You're not who you were back then."

When she took a breath, it wobbled. "She's still part of me."

Justin's face came to mind, his hurt expression as he accused me of using him. "I understand."

I woke up Saturday morning with that feeling in my stomach like I'd done something really, really wrong. It came back in a flood of anger and hurt—Eli showing up at Houlihan's, Connor's insistence on us talking about what happened a year ago. Almost exactly a year ago.

All night, I'd pushed Connor's phone calls into voice mail. I hadn't wanted to deal with him, but in the light of the morning, I could see how he'd been doing what he thought would help. How he wanted what was best for me.

I quietly buzzed through my morning routine—a shower, blow-drying my hair, fifteen minutes of choosing and changing my outfit, followed by three minutes of makeup. Then I snuck downstairs to the kitchen for a quick bite to silence my rumbling stomach.

"You're up early," Dad called from his office.

I jumped. "You scared me."

"I gathered." He maneuvered from behind his desk, through the open French doors, to the kitchen. "Where you off to?"

"The Rosses."

Dad frowned at the clock. "At eight?"

"Connor and I are having breakfast."

Dad glanced at my hand halfway into the Cookie Crisp box.

"I needed a little something. The line at First Watch gets kinda long sometimes."

He nodded. "Have an omelet for me, okay?"

"Yeah, sure." I couldn't end the conversation like that, on a lie about a breakfast date, and I hunted for a quick conversation topic before I rushed out the door. "You and Mom have fun last night?"

"Mm-hmm. The movie stunk, but your mom seemed to enjoy it."

"Well, she's a chick."

He smiled. "True." Then his smile faded and he cleared his throat. Looked like this wouldn't be as quick a conversation as I'd hoped. "Skylar, when you came in the other day, your mom and I were arguing, and I know how unsettling that must feel. But please let me assure you that your mom and I are fine. We're still working through things, but we're fine."

I repackaged the cereal with care. "Okay."

"Arguing is normal. There's always going to be tension between people, but it doesn't mean one of us is going to leave or that we're getting a divorce."

"How do you know for sure?" I asked. I thought of Heather and Guy, of how she thought she'd loved him at the time but now didn't think so. "How do you know it's the right relationship?"

Dad frowned. "Are you speaking specifically about your mom and me, or is this a broader question?"

"Broader," I admitted.

"Well, I guess you don't always know. Until the relationship is tested. As hard as the tests are, that's when you find out if you're in it for the long haul or if it's time to call it quits." He smiled. "Your mom and I are in it for the long haul."

It warmed my heart to hear him say that. I pecked his cheek. "I'm glad."

"Enjoy breakfast," he called after me.

I hoped I would.

Connor's voice sounded gravelly but decently awake when he answered his cell. "I didn't know when I'd hear from you again."

"Yeah, about that. I'm really sorry."

"Don't be," he said through a yawn. "I shouldn't have taken you to that parking garage."

"You were trying to do what you thought was best. I just wasn't in the mood to see it that way."

He didn't speak, but I could hear something kinda scratchy, as if he rubbed his unshaven chin. "I want to ask you something, but I don't want to make you mad again."

I pulled alongside his curb. "Go ahead."

"Really?"

"Why not?" I shut off the ignition and relaxed in my seat. "Hit me with it."

"Is it that you don't remember much about that night, or that you remember but don't want to talk about it?"

Pictures flashed in my mind—Eli's jealous eyes on Aaron and me, Aaron's grin when he handed me my doctored drink, the blur of faces as he led me upstairs.

"Sometimes it feels like I remember every detail." I

pressed my fingertips to my forehead. "I wish they'd just go away."

"Me too," Connor said in the same gentle voice he used when speaking to Owen.

I sighed. "You hungry?"

"It's too early to be hungry."

"Well, I'm parked on your street and I'm starving."

"Oh yeah?" A second later, Connor's blinds raised and I saw an outline of him. "How long have you been out there?"

"Just a couple minutes. You wanna go to First Watch or something?"

"I don't know. You think Eli and Molly will be there?"

"Marin. And I doubt it. Too early for him."

"If he's there, we'll get our pancakes to go."

"Deal."

"I'll be down in ten."

"Ten? How long can it possibly take to pull on exercise shorts and a T-shirt?"

"Bye," Connor said and hung up on me.

It felt nice to have things resolved and comfortable between us once again. No matter how short-lived it might be.

It'd barely been five minutes when Connor jogged out to the car. He smacked my forehead with a kiss. "My mom says hello."

"Was the kiss also from your mom?"

"No, that was all me." He buckled his seat belt. "Thanks for coming over. For suggesting breakfast."

"Yeah, sure." I grazed the key with my fingers but didn't turn it.

"What's wrong?"

I glanced at him. "You're right that I should talk about that night. I'm just not ready."

His hand cupped my knee. "That's fine."

"I don't know when I will be."

"I'm here whenever."

The thought brought a smile to my face.

21

I'd been at the mall most of the morning, shopping for nothing in particular. As I realized I'd somehow walked past Fossil, a familiar and unwelcome voice said, "Skylar?"

I turned to find Jodi in line at Auntie Anne's Pretzels. She abandoned her spot to come see me. "What's going on?"

I dangled my bags. "Shopping."

"Right. Me too." She held out her unburdened arms. "Unsuccessfully, though."

"You looking for something specific?"

"A dress for Heather's wedding. I found one I really liked at Nordstrom, but they didn't have my size and couldn't promise it for another four to six weeks."

"Bummer." I took a step backward, mentally kicking myself for wandering down this way. "Well, I'll—"

"You want a pretzel?" Jodi smiled. "I'm not really hungry, but they always smell so good. Remember how in eighth grade you'd always get cinnamon and sugar and I'd get a salted one, and then we'd split them?"

"Kinda." I moved another step backward.

She either didn't notice that I wanted out of this conversation or didn't care. "I heard you and Connor are back together."

179

I blinked. "Yeah, I know. I told you."

"Oh, right. Well, I think it's great."

"No you don't." I couldn't believe I'd just said that. I shifted. "At least, I wouldn't have thought it was great if it was you guys."

Jodi's smile grew. "Okay, so I overstated it with 'great.' You know, I wish I could be more like you. Just say whatever I felt and not care what others think."

I snorted. That hardly described me. Maybe once upon a time I'd been like that, before Aaron. Before I'd become a Christian . . . But it shouldn't work like that, should it? Embracing God should have made me *more* authentic, not less.

"Can we talk?" Jodi interrupted my train of thought. "Like a real conversation? I feel like we haven't had one since . . ." She shrugged. "Since you started dating Eli, I guess."

I hesitated.

Jodi apparently noticed. "I don't need us to be friends again, Skylar. I don't expect that. It'd just be nice to resolve things between us. Before I leave town."

That didn't sound so bad, a little closure on everything that had transpired in the last year.

"There's a Panera downstairs," I said.

Jodi looked happy, but like she didn't want to show it. As if her happiness might spook me. "Okay, sure."

As we headed down the mall, I imagined we looked to everyone else like two normal high school girls out for a day of shopping. Last summer, they'd have been right. We used to giggle as we browsed, making eyes at the college guys who'd come home for the summer. It seemed a lifetime ago, which I hoped meant I'd made more progress toward changing, toward reinvention, than I felt I had.

In the short line at Panera's bakery, I assessed my options for coffee drinks tasting nothing like coffee. Behind me, Jodi groaned.

I turned and found her looking straight ahead. "What?"

"Sarah Humphrey," Jodi said under her breath. "I totally forgot she works here."

I frowned at Sarah, who hadn't seemed to notice us. Even though it'd been nearly two years since Jodi lopped off her ponytail (and, okay, Jodi *might* have had some help from me), Sarah still wore her hair in a blunt, short style. Her hair looked nicer now than it had all those years she wore it long. Really, we'd done her a favor.

"I feel horrible for what I did to her," Jodi said.

"Maybe you should tell her that."

"I did back in the spring, but it's only seemed to make her hate me more. And of course she's slowly but surely trying to poison Alexis against me."

I tried to connect the dots but couldn't. "Are her and Alexis friends?"

"Well, you know, Sarah's boyfriend is Nate. That tall, lurchy guy who hangs out with Aaron."

"Aaron Robinson?" My voice cracked like a twelve-year-old boy's. I hated how his name kept springing into conversations. I had no chance to guard my reaction.

"Yeah." Jodi looked at me funny. "You didn't know that? Don't you remember when they crashed my party last year? Sarah's the reason they came. According to Alexis, they came to 'teach me a lesson,' but I barely saw her that night, so I've got no idea what she's talking about."

The customer who'd blocked us from Sarah's view shifted to the cash register, exposing us. Sarah stared, her pretty face drawn into a hard expression.

"Hey, Sarah," Jodi said in a friendly yet not-too-chipper voice. "How's it going?"

Sarah didn't move a muscle.

"Um, okay. Well, I'd like a vanilla cappuccino—"

Sarah stalked away.

"Let's just go." Jodi tugged at my sleeve. "I don't want to deal with her."

But Sarah turning her back on Jodi—on us—had lit something inside me. "No. I've been looking at those pumpkin muffins, and I'm gonna have one."

The other bakery worker, middle-aged and likely a manager of some sort, finished at the cash register and noticed us. "Has someone helped you girls?" He glanced around, as if he'd find Sarah.

"There was someone here," I said. "A girl with short blonde hair, but she just walked away."

He frowned. "I'm so sorry about that. What can I get for you gals?"

"I'll have a black-and-white latte and a pumpkin muffin. My friend would like a vanilla cappuccino."

"Sure thing."

He rang us up, slid my muffin across the counter, and after another apology, assured us our coffees would be right out.

"You probably just got her in trouble," Jodi whispered as we slid into a table for two.

"Good," I said in a normal voice. The place crawled with people. No way could Sarah hear this conversation. "What's wrong with her? I mean, yeah, you probably shouldn't have cut off her hair—"

Jodi sighed and nodded.

"—but that was a long time ago, you've apologized, and . . ." Ugh. How'd that saying of my mom's go? The one about the pot calling the kettle black? That sounded pretty close, although my mom's pots were cobalt Le Creusets and our teakettle was stainless steel. "And I guess I shouldn't come down so hard on Sarah when I haven't been the picture of forgiveness."

Jodi's eyes widened. "Well . . ." She didn't seem to know what to say. "Don't worry about it. I never really expected you to forgive me for everything I did this year."

"But everything turned out okay. I mean, Connor and I are . . . you know. Great. And even if things hadn't turned out like I wanted, I'm still supposed to forgive you." I sighed. "It turns out I really suck at forgiveness."

"Me too. Especially when it comes to forgiving myself for everything."

"Yeah." I cut my muffin in half and pushed part of it her way.

She smiled. "Thanks."

Two coffees in paper cups slammed onto our table. Sarah bared her teeth at us in some sort of fake smile. "Drink up. Made 'em myself." She stalked away.

A giggle bubbled up from inside me as I looked at our coffees. "Okay, I'm so not drinking that."

"Yeah, there's no way."

We smiled at each other. Maybe we really could be friends now. If we could get beyond her having a mad crush on my boyfriend.

I picked at my muffin. "Have you talked to Connor recently?" Last Saturday, when I'd asked him about Jodi, he'd told me they weren't talking, but I couldn't resist hearing her answer.

"No," she relieved me by saying. "I told you, I'm out. I leave for Vanderbilt in a month, and you guys . . . Well, things are how they're supposed to be. I didn't always understand you two being together, but I see it now."

"Do you? Because sometimes I'm not sure I do."

"Remember the night we met him? You hated him."

"Oh, I didn't hate him," I said, embarrassed.

"You did! You thought he was so obnoxious. I could tell."

"Well, maybe a little. But mostly I was just leery of guys. It'd been—" It'd been less than twenty-four hours since Aaron roofied me. But of course Jodi didn't know that.

"It'd been what?" she asked.

"It'd been a weird night."

"I'll say. I couldn't believe it when I found out you were dating Eli. When Alexis called and told me, I thought she must be playing some sort of prank."

"Unfortunately, no."

Jodi cocked her head. "Yeah, so what's the deal? And don't give me that line about his Land Rover. We both know your dad would've bought you a fleet of Land Rovers if you cared so much. So why'd you really get together?"

I shrugged, wishing myself thousands of miles away. On a stretch of beach in Kauai where no one knew who Eli or Aaron were. Where no one would ask me questions.

But I'd come back for this reason—to remember. To remember so I could move on.

I remembered sitting at First Watch with Eli the morning after, same as I had with Connor just a few days ago. "I can't believe I let him get away with it," I had said, doing my best not to cry into the pancakes he'd bought me that I'd barely touched. I'd eaten enough to remove the acidic vomit taste from my mouth, then stopped.

Eli covered my hand with his own. "It's not your fault."

"I drank way too much." I pressed my fingertips to my temples. I'd had hangovers before, but never like this one. "I don't know why. I guess I was trying to impress him."

"I think it was more than drinking."

I cracked open my eyes, letting in light that felt like a knife to my brain. "What do you mean?"

In a hushed voice, he said, "I think he maybe drugged you."

"Drugged me?" My mushy brain made vain attempts to process this. "Like, he put something in my drink?"

Eli nodded.

"Are you just making that up, or did you actually see something?"

"I saw something."

"What?"

"Pills." He swallowed. "Little white ones."

"Like roofies? Aren't roofies white?"

Eli nodded.

"And you saw him put them in my drink?"

He swallowed and nodded again.

I buried my head in my hands. "How could I have been so stupid? I'm always *so* careful about who I get drinks from."

"You're not stupid," Eli said, taking my hand. "You're wonderful."

"Skylar?"

I blinked a few times, finding myself not at First Watch with Eli but at Panera with Jodi. Between spacing out and now, my head had started to throb.

Jodi seemed to be waiting, and I remembered now that she'd asked about me and Eli, about why I'd started dating him.

"I guess it was a right-time, right-place kinda thing." Honest but vague. My specialty these days. "I regret it. And I'm sorry I dated him when I told you I wouldn't."

Jodi shrugged, but the shadows on her face told me how I'd hurt her. "Like you said, it was a long time ago. And everything's worked out okay."

I picked at my muffin, no longer hungry. I wished for a warm, soothing drink of my latte but didn't dare. "You think she spit in them?" I asked, nodding at our untouched cups.

She smiled. "Probably. And then drugged them."

The back of my neck tingled. I waited until I was sure I could keep my voice even and casual. "Why do you say that?"

Had that sounded casual enough?

She laughed. "Oh, I hear rumors about that guy she's dating. That he's the one to go to if you wanna get hooked up."

"That guy she's dating," I said slowly. "Like, Aaron's friend?"

Jodi nodded. "That's the one."

22

Since my conversation with Jodi that morning, I couldn't think about anything but Sarah's boyfriend, the go-to guy. Could I assume Aaron got the roofie from him? When Aaron came to talk to me, was the pill in his pocket, waiting for just the right time?

And why did this make any difference to me? It didn't change what'd happened, or who I was now. It meant nothing.

And yet the questions lingered.

"You okay?"

I blinked and forced my mind back to the here and now—the waning sunlight, the hard bleachers, whining cicadas.

I matched Amy's wide smile. "Yeah. Just zoned out, I guess."

"You've been doing that a lot tonight." She gestured to the field. "Connor's on third."

Sure enough. Last I remembered, there'd still been several batters in line before him. "Oh. How'd I miss that?"

"Is there something you want to talk about?"

I shrugged and peeled my hands off the bleacher. They ached from gripping the edge so hard. I must have looked like a psycho sitting there with white knuckles and glazed eyes.

I double-checked our surroundings. Two other wives and sets of kids had come to watch the game, but the women stood at the base of the bleachers, involved in their own conversation. Their kids, plus Cameron and Curtis, screamed and ran and did all the other things kids did.

"I assume you know things with Jodi and me have been kind of weird for a while. I saw her at the mall today and we talked."

"How was it?"

"Okay. It'd been about a year since we had a conversation without either of us being . . . What's the word?"

"Snarky?"

"Sure, yeah. We talked through some stuff that needed to be talked out. I don't know if we'll ever be friends exactly, but it was nice to get everything on the table." Or almost everything.

Amy nodded, her eyes still on the game. When she started clapping, I did too. I didn't know what had happened, but Connor crossed home plate.

"God doesn't call us to be friends with everyone," Amy said. "Of course it'd be nice if you and Jodi could be friends again, but I'm very happy to hear you're at peace with each other."

She always articulated things so much better than me. No fair.

"Peace is a good way to put it," I said. "I don't feel angry with her. Maybe if we met each other for the first time today, we could be friends, but too much has happened between us. She knows way too many embarrassing things about me."

Amy gave me a closed-mouth smile, as if amused. "Sometimes those are the best people to have as friends. They understand you in ways others don't because they lived with you through those hard, weird, and embarrassing times."

I sighed. "You totally should've had a daughter. You're really good at this stuff."

Now her smile faltered. "I'd have liked a daughter."

Amy had never before said it so plainly, but we'd had enough conversations that I could have guessed it. Why'd I have to say something so dumb? "I'm really sorry. I didn't mean to—"

"Don't. I know how you meant it." She took a deep breath. "And you've been around our family long enough that it's probably time I told you."

I squeezed my eyes shut. Great. I'd apparently rammed my foot further in my mouth than I'd originally thought.

"I'd appreciate it if you kept this between us, though."

I nodded. "But Amy, if you don't want to tell me, you don't have to." If anyone understood wanting secrecy, I did.

"I don't mind." Amy's face took on a determined expression. "Brian and I lost a baby between Chris and Cameron. A little girl. Abigail. When I went in at twenty weeks for a sonogram, I assumed they'd tell me she looked good and healthy, same as they'd done with Connor and Chris." Amy took a wobbly breath. "But instead the technician poked around for a long time, and then she called in my doctor. He said it looked like our baby had a chromosomal abnormality, trisomy 18, but they'd need to do an amnio to be sure. When the results came back positive, he said if she made it to full-term, the chances of seeing her first birthday were less than 10 percent, and we should decide if we wanted to continue the pregnancy."

I swallowed and tried to think of something noncliché to say to Amy. When she'd regained control of her vocal cords, I still hadn't come up with anything.

"Connor and Chris had both been such easy, by-the-book pregnancies. I just sat there and stared at the doctor, thinking this couldn't be happening. And Brian, sweet, dear Brian, said we needed to go home and talk it over. I looked that doctor in the eye and told him nobody was coming near my baby. Of course, it's not that Brian *wanted* to abort the baby, but he worried she'd cause health problems for me. The guilt of aborting her would've killed me."

Amy took another breath. "I had a couple more months with her. Terrifying months. All I wanted to eat was pancakes. I dreamt at night about pancakes, but I forced myself to eat healthy stuff. Lots of salad and chicken and whole grains. As if somehow I could . . ."

She bit her trembling lower lip and I reached for her hand. When she gripped mine, she squeezed my fingers so hard it brought back memories of Abbie laboring with Owen.

"Around thirty weeks, Abigail stopped moving. They couldn't find a heartbeat, and I knew even before they induced labor that we'd lost her. She was so tiny, barely two pounds. Brian and I held her and cried, and then hours later when my parents brought Connor and Chris to visit, we held them and cried. Chris was two and didn't understand much of what was going on, but Connor . . ." Amy's fingers danced along her neck. "He was devastated. He hugged me so tight, sobbing that he was sorry, as if he'd done something wrong."

She wiped away tears and took a deep breath. "Sometimes Brian and I talk about Abigail, but not often. On her birthday every year, we go out for pancakes. The older boys understand why, and Cameron's starting to piece it together, but mostly he and Curtis know it's a rough day for Mommy and pancakes help me feel better."

"I'm really sorry," I said. Sorry I'd dredged it up, that I'd made Amy feel bad. "I think you're really brave to talk about it."

Amy laughed a little, still raspy with emotion. "I don't know if *brave* is the right word."

"It takes a lot to share a piece of yourself like that." I swallowed back tears of my own. "You're brave."

Amy considered this. "I never *like* talking about Abigail, but over the years I've gotten more comfortable with it. It helps that it's such a popular name. I've gotten used to having lots of Abigails around me." She gave a sad smile. "It makes it extra special having you and your sister around so much." She sighed. "I still always lose it when I think of Connor at the hospital." She smiled at him in the outfield. "He's always had such a tender heart."

"How long was it?" I asked. "Before talking about it got easier, I mean."

Amy frowned as she thought. "You know, it's never gotten 'easy,' but the first time was by far the worst. Abigail and her little life had been cramped in my brain all those months as I stubbornly tried to figure things out for myself." Amy shrugged. "I don't think I really started to heal until I forced myself to talk about it, to share the details. I hate to think of what might have happened, of the stunted person I might have become, if I hadn't opened up."

"Your mom told me about Abigail tonight."

Connor looked up from his turtle sundae. "Really?"

"Yeah. I stuck my foot in my mouth by saying she should've had a daughter, and then she told me."

He scooped his cherry into my cup. "That's a really big deal. You should feel honored."

"Do you remember much of what happened?"

"Not really. I was only four, so . . ." Connor shrugged. "I wish I remembered better. It's this really huge thing that happened in our family, and I feel a little guilty for not feeling affected."

"Like you said, you were four. The only thing I remember from that age was when Abbie and I were taking a bath together and she mistook the bathtub for a toilet."

Connor made a face. "That's disgusting."

"Tell me about it." I stirred the soupy remains of my custard. "I kinda wish you'd told me about Abigail. I felt really stupid bringing up something so painful for your mom."

"It's not mine to tell."

I turned that statement over in my mind, along with Amy's words of wisdom. Was it stunting me, not talking about Aaron? Was I hindering God from working in my life? I didn't want that. I wanted to be over this.

"I think I'm ready to talk. About what happened at Jodi's." I swallowed. I didn't want him to make a big deal out of it. I just wanted to lay out the events of that night as I remembered and let the healing begin.

Connor turned to me as casually as if I'd said we should see a movie later. "Go ahead."

23

On July 14, a year ago yesterday, my friends and I showed up for Jodi's party fashionably late. Alexis had wanted to come earlier. She cared much more about being there for every gossip-soaked second than she did about making an entrance.

When she spotted us, Jodi charged in from the kitchen. "Where have you guys been?" She talked way too loud, clearly several drinks ahead of us.

"Have we missed anything?" Alexis asked.

Jodi rolled her eyes. "No. I swear this'll be the last party I throw. It sucks having to be here from the beginning." Her eyes accused me. "You said you'd be here an hour ago."

I shrugged. "I thought we'd leave the Plaza earlier."

"They practically kicked us out," Lisa said. "The store clerks were irritated. You could totally tell."

I accepted the cigarette Eli offered me, ignoring how he'd unnecessarily brushed his fingertips against my wrist. "The sign says they're open till nine. Why should I rush out of there? Hello, it's their job."

Now Eli's fingertips grazed my lower back. "Absolutely."

"I need a drink." I wove through the crowded room, escaping him.

"So you left at nine," Jodi said as she walked next to me. "What've you been doing for the last hour?"

"Getting ready." Did she think I'd dressed like this for an afternoon of shopping?

She leaned against the kitchen counter as I grabbed myself a red plastic cup. "So, Danny's here."

I didn't have to look to know she'd rolled her eyes. "Yeah?"

"He's being all sulky and annoying. I wish he'd just leave." She refreshed her beer as I sipped mine. "Him being all pathetic is making me look pathetic for dating him so long."

Though if he'd acted normal, she'd have been miffed about that as well.

"Well, you can't blame him," I said. "You *are* pretty fabulous."

"Who's fabulous?" Eli leaned close as he filled his cup.

"Jodi."

"Of course she is." He winked at her. "Dated me, right?"

Jodi rolled her eyes again, but a smile tugged at the corners of her mouth.

Through the breakfast bar and sea of people, I spotted Lisa waving me over. I left Jodi and Eli to their conversation and maneuvered my way to Lisa. She leaned against an ugly but very expensive sage wingback chair. John's arms circled her waist, but he was turned away from us, talking to some guy I didn't recognize.

"Guess who's here!" Lisa yelled over the thumping bass.

I followed her line of vision and saw him, the guy we'd dubbed TDH—Tall, Dark, and Hot. We'd gone to a handful of parties since the summer started and seen him at most.

He'd seen me—I knew he had—but TDH had yet to make a move. Maybe tonight would be the night.

He caught my eye then, and I held his gaze for a second. Tonight his six-plus feet of yummy boyness was clad in cargo shorts and a black graphic print tee meant to look like he'd had it forever.

I turned back to Lisa and shrugged. "He may be cute"— hello, understatement—"but I still refuse to talk to him."

"*This* is why you don't have a boyfriend. A modern girl's got to be willing to make the first move."

"I'm old-fashioned," I said wryly.

Lisa looked back at TDH. "He's totally into you. Can't you offer him a friendly smile so he knows it's cool to come talk to you? Sometimes guys need a little encouragement."

John had dropped out of his conversation halfway through Lisa's statement. "Who are we talking about?"

"That guy by the stereo."

"Which guy by the stereo? There's about a billion guys by the stereo."

"The one with dark hair and skin—"

"About half of them have dark hair and skin."

"The really cute one—"

"The really cute one?" John asked, and Lisa winced at her mistake. John didn't have a jealous streak—he had a jealous *mile*.

"*Skylar* thinks he's cute," Lisa said.

I doubted this specification would fix anything, but John turned to me. "What about Eli?"

"What about Eli?"

"You're toying with my boy's heart. You realize that, right?"

I rolled my eyes. "Please." But that guilty burn started in my stomach, the one that sometimes kept me awake at night because I knew I'd been leading Eli on.

"He knows our situation." I tipped back my cup, hoping to chase away my conscience. "Jodi'd kill me."

Lisa snorted. "She'd do worse. She'd make your life so miserable, you'd wish she *had* killed you. I can only imagine how your hair would look short. And speaking of which . . ." Lisa nodded at Sarah Humphrey, who lurked around Mrs. Starr's china cabinet. "What's she doing here?"

I wrinkled my nose. "She probably thinks Jodi and Danny are still together and she's here to do some damage."

"She's got a boyfriend. Actually, she hangs with Mr. TDH himself."

"Skylar!"

I turned toward Jodi, who'd yelled my name from the kitchen.

"Change the song, would ya? I *hate* this song." Now she looked at Danny, and I vaguely remembered this being "their song." Danny didn't react, just returned to his game of quarters.

I normally wouldn't have involved myself in one of Jodi's post-breakup spats, but it gave me a handy excuse to walk by TDH. I kept my gaze fixed on the stereo beyond him, but I could feel him watching me.

"Hi," he said, his voice clear and smooth.

I tapped SKIP, then glanced at him. "Hi."

"Masterful," Lisa said as I returned to her and John. "He hasn't taken his eyes off you."

"I don't like you watching him so much," John grumbled.

Lisa glared at him. "Like you don't help Eli with girls when the two of you are out."

"Eli doesn't chase girls anymore." He slanted me a glare. "Wanna guess why?"

I shrugged and drained the contents of my cup. "Not my problem." And after the next beer I downed, hopefully I'd feel as careless as I sounded.

"You want another?" Lisa said. "I'm gonna go get one."

I handed her my cup. "Yeah, sure."

John waited until she'd left to say to me, "Skylar, I'm being serious about Eli. He's got it bad for you. You need to either cut him loose or give him a chance." He seemed to hesitate before adding, "And I'm saying that for your own good."

I glanced toward the breakfast bar, but Eli had moved. He now stood in the eat-in kitchen, chatting with some blonde chick who'd blocked him in and appeared to be talking incessantly. He looked past her and smiled at me.

I frowned at John. "What do you mean, for my own good?"

"You know how he is. You've seen his temper."

I opened my mouth to respond but got interrupted by Jodi's and Alexis's squeals as they pounced on the couch and danced wildly.

"Come on, Skylar!" Jodi said.

She sounded drunk, drunk, drunk. And I'd have to be as well to get up there.

I pulled a cigarette from the pack in my back pocket. "There's no way," I said to John.

He grinned, watching my crazy, stupid friends. "I don't know. You'd definitely get what's-his-face's attention."

"You think so?" I turned and saw TDH still watching me. "I don't know. I think he's got a thing for Lisa."

John frowned and scanned the crowd. "Where'd she go, anyway?" He walked off toward the kitchen without another word to me.

I bit back a smile and watched Jodi's long blonde hair fly through the air. Man, she'd wake up with a headache.

"You know, I've been watching you the last couple weeks."

I turned to see him standing where John had been. If possible, he looked even better up close.

I exhaled cigarette smoke. "Oh, yeah?"

"You're friends with those girls, right?" He indicated Alexis and Jodi with his drink.

"Yeah."

"Weird. You seem so much older than them." He took a sip and studied me. "There's definitely something different about you."

I hoped I hid my smile better than Jodi had earlier in the kitchen with Eli. "Maybe," I said with a shrug.

"You know what else I've noticed?" He leaned closer. "Wherever you are, he is too."

I looked in the direction he nodded. The blonde girl still had Eli trapped. He bobbed his head politely as she prattled on and on. And on. When he noticed Aaron and me, he frowned.

"He's a friend of mine," I said.

"Hmm. So I'm not gonna step on any toes if I get you a drink?"

I shook my head. I wanted to look away from him, to not look too enthralled, but I couldn't lower my gaze.

"Be right back," he said.

"Wow," Jodi breathed in my ear, her dancing routine apparently over. "How gorgeous is he?"

We watched him walk into the kitchen. From our post at the ugly sage chair, we could see only from his shoulders down. Stupid cabinets.

"What's his name?" she asked.

"I don't know yet."

"Of course, he could be named Archibald Frederick the Third and I wouldn't complain."

I smiled, then glanced at Eli. Instead of watching me, he'd trained his focus on the kitchen. And I'd bet money on who.

"Gosh, Sarah Humphrey's here?" Jodi hissed. I followed her line of sight, which also led to the kitchen. There Sarah stood, with her flapper-girl haircut and too-long-to-be-real eyelashes, which she batted at a very tall guy in a black shirt. A tall, dark, and hot guy, I'd guess.

"What is she, stupid?" Jodi said, her voice pure venom. "If she even thinks about taking him from you, I'll make it a military cut next time."

Sarah cocked her head and passed him her cup, beaming with a big, fake smile.

I turned to Jodi. "Well, if he's easily persuaded by someone like Sarah Humphrey, I doubt I want him anyway."

Jodi took a break from shooting mental daggers at Sarah to give me an exasperated look. "You're so practical. It's no fun."

She scanned the living room, as if searching for someone.

"Seen anyone good tonight?" I asked.

"You definitely landed the pick of the litter. But the night's young."

I nodded to Eli. "Eli's looking pretty miserable. Maybe you could save him from the wordy girl and do a little reigniting."

"I'm not nearly drunk enough for that," Jodi said with a laugh. "Besides, he's only got eyes for you these days."

I didn't answer. My guy had finally broken away from Sarah's clutches and moved toward Jodi and me, balancing three cups in his fingers.

He winked at Jodi. "Grabbed yours for you too."

"What a sweetheart," Jodi said. She gave him a flirtatious smile and slipped away with her drink.

I accepted the cup and stared into his dark pools of eyes. "You forgot to tell me your name."

"Aaron," he said. "Robinson. And yours is Skylar, right?"

I nodded.

"I've never known a Skylar before."

"There aren't many of us out there. I guess my mom wanted to name me Skylark but my dad said no. Skylar was a compromise."

"A good compromise." He smiled, showing off his straight, white teeth.

"I don't think I've seen you around Shawnee Mission," I said, taking the first drink of my beer.

And we began exchanging information. He'd just graduated from one of the Blue Valley schools and was headed to Florida State in the fall. That's where his dad lived, and he couldn't wait. It was just him and his mom around the house, and she'd become super controlling since the divorce.

"I just want out of here," Aaron said.

"Totally," I agreed and drained my cup.

He got me a refill, then started asking questions about me. When I told him my dad was P. M. Hoyt of P. M. Hoyt Construction, he was appropriately impressed. "I see their trailers all over," he said.

"Yeah." I shrugged as if it were no big deal that my dad owned the largest construction company in the metro area.

As I talked about my friends, I felt my eyelids growing heavy. Why did I feel so tired? I'd slept in until about noon. I should've felt fine. I had a hard time focusing on Aaron's face, and noises around me seemed louder, sharper. I gripped my nearly empty cup. Talking to Aaron had made me nervous and I must have drunk too quickly. That's all this was.

"So, you should call me sometime." Aaron tugged my cell phone from where it peeked out of my front pocket. "You know, when you get tired of all these high school boys. How should I put myself in your directory? 'Cute Guy I Met at Party?'"

"Way too vague," I said. "I'll never remember which one you were."

Aaron laughed, and it seemed really loud. He'd been drinking a lot too.

Nearby, Jodi cackled at something, then stumbled into an end table and sent a framed family picture tumbling to the ground. At the sound of breaking glass, she laughed even harder. How much had *she* had to drink?

"You're not like your friends," Aaron said.

I looked up at him, finding him very close to my face. He brushed his mouth against mine, and when the room swirled, I grabbed hold of his shirt to keep from falling. My stomach churned. I so didn't want to puke on this guy.

"Let's find someplace a little more quiet," he whispered.

I nodded. Quiet sounded good.

I felt a weight on top of me. When I managed to open my eyes, I saw Aaron. Where were we? The room was dark except the blinking numbers of an alarm clock. The Starrs' guest bedroom? I'd never been allowed in here.

I realized Aaron was kissing me. My mouth felt furry, and I'd never wanted a drink of water so bad in all my life.

Aaron pulled back and looked at me. "What?"

Had I said something? "I'm thirsty," I said. "And . . ." My stomach felt horrible, and I just knew I'd throw up in another minute. I started to cry. "Please let me go. I'm thirsty."

A beam of light sliced across the room. "What are you doing? Get off her!"

Lots of shouting. My eyes felt too heavy to open. Was this a dream or was it real?

There were two voices. One I recognized—Eli—and one I didn't. Both sounded angry. I couldn't understand what they said to each other. I couldn't understand anything, just the angry volume of their words and the way they took up the whole room, letting me fade away.

The bare skin of my lower back tingled with contact. Eli's words were warm in my ear. "You're okay."

"What's going on?" Had I said the words out loud? Had Eli even understood?

"You're okay. I've got you."

He drew me close, and I recalled being a little girl—when I'd fall asleep on the couch during a movie, my dad always lifted me as though I weighed nothing and carried me to the security of my warm, comfy bed.

I snuggled against Eli's chest. He'd take me home. He'd let me sleep. He'd keep me safe.

Connor's fingers laced through mine. He hadn't touched me while I talked, just sat there and listened while I purged myself of every detail. My body felt more relaxed, as if it'd been tense this whole year, winding tighter and tighter each time I pushed away the memories of that night.

"Is that all you remember?" Connor asked.

I hugged my knees to my chest. "Pretty much. The next morning I woke up in the backseat of Eli's Land Rover. He was sleeping up front. It was around 7:00, I think. The sun was up, anyway."

"And then Eli told you about the roofies?"

"Not until breakfast. I threw up for a while in some shrubs, and then he took me to First Watch. That's when he told me about Aaron and the drugs and everything."

"Did he tell you anything about what he saw when he came into the room?"

I shook my head. "But I didn't ask. I was afraid I didn't want to know." I glanced at Connor out of the corner of my eye. He stared into the street, which was quiet with the late hour. "You think that was dumb. That I should've asked."

Connor turned to me. "Stop taking every question I ask as judgment. I'm just trying to help you figure out what really happened that night."

"So you still think Eli might have lied."

He shrugged. "You didn't say anything that made me rule it out. What still doesn't make sense to me is if he really did see Aaron drug your drink, why didn't he stop you from drinking it? Why wait until Aaron had already taken you upstairs to take action?"

I turned these questions over in my mind. "But why lie about it?"

"Lots of reasons. To make it okay that he barged into the room. So he'd look like a hero. In hopes that you'd start thinking of him as more than a friend."

"I'm glad he barged into the room." I shuddered to think of Aaron's weight on me. "Whatever his reasons."

Connor squeezed my hand. "Me too."

"Do you think it's possible . . ." I didn't want to think it, much less say it. "Do you think maybe Eli drugged me?"

Connor inhaled and exhaled slowly. "I've wondered that, but I'm pretty sure he didn't."

I released a breath I didn't know I'd been holding. "Why?"

"Why give Aaron a black eye a couple weeks ago if Eli's the one who drugged you?"

I considered this. "But also, why punch him if Eli's lying about the roofies in the first place?"

"Same reason he might've lied to begin with. In hopes of winning you back with warped chivalry."

My head spun with all this. It'd been hard enough recalling that night, searching my brain for every last detail. To consider that the realities of what happened at the party might not line up with what I'd been told . . . Well, it was a little too much.

I sagged against Connor. "Let's not talk about it anymore tonight."

"Okay." He tucked his arm around me. "We'll just sit here until you're ready to go home."

We stayed there long after Sheridan's shut off its lights.

24

When I woke up late the next morning, my body felt refreshed, as if I'd slept a hundred years. Peace nested in my soul, and a delicious sense of freedom invigorated me.

I'd told him. Connor knew everything, yet things between us were still good. He hadn't been freaked out by my sordid past. If anything, he seemed further endeared.

I grinned at the ceiling. "Thank you, God, for a boyfriend who doesn't mind me being a little needy." I plopped my bare feet on the floor, eager to be up and about and alive. I didn't hear the commotion downstairs until I stepped out of my room.

"You gave up that right two weeks ago when you broke up with me!" Abbie said.

"It's not like I stopped caring about you," Chris said. "You know that—"

"How would I know that? I said, 'I love you,' and you said, 'I don't think we should see each other anymore.' What was I supposed to think?"

Silence. Chris argued slowly. Lots of pauses while he dwelled on the perfect response. This drove my impatient sister crazy.

I grabbed my bathrobe off the back of my bedroom door.

I barely ever used it, but in case I needed to go down and rescue Abbie (or Chris, for that matter), I wanted to be prepared. No way did I want to parade around in front of Chris in my summer pj's.

I moved toward the edge of the stairs in time to hear Chris's response.

"Despite what you may think, I *do* care about you. And I'm worried about what I'm seeing. You've been really different since Owen was born—"

"Oh, have I? That's because I have a baby, Chris. Why's everyone so surprised that I'm a different person these days? I don't have the option of being who I was."

"And I get that, but—"

"No you don't! If you got it, you wouldn't be stupid enough to come over here and imply that something's wrong with me for not showing more emotion about us breaking up. Look, I thought I loved you, I was clearly wrong. I'm over it. I've moved on. And now you can move out the door." My sister planted her hand firmly on Chris's chest, pushing him backward toward the front door.

"I just need to know you're talking to somebody. You used to tell me everything, and I want to make sure you still have someone—"

"That's none of your business. You made sure of it." Abbie pointed at the door. "Leave."

Chris studied my sister for a moment, giving her a long look that I could read even from the top of the stairwell—regret.

Abbie either didn't see or didn't care. She slammed the door in his face, then marched across the tiled entryway and out of view.

She banged around in the kitchen for a few minutes. I waited for the cupboard doors to be silent before I ventured downstairs.

"Hey," I said, trying to sound casual.

Abbie looked up from her seat at the counter. "What's with the robe?"

"Oh, just . . . cold." I pulled the orange juice from the refrigerator. "Mom and Dad gone?"

"Yep."

I glanced at the clock—9:58. "Owen napping?"

"Uh-huh."

"Anything else going on?"

Abbie flipped the page of her J.Crew catalog. "Not a thing."

A pretty girl, blonde and willowy, answered the door. "Hi." She turned her smile to full wattage. "Come on in."

"Thanks." I stepped inside the strange house. The inside looked as typically suburban as the outside—lots of taupe walls and neutral-colored furniture. All the furniture had been lived on, but not enough to replace it. Unless you were Teri Hoyt, who I'd bet had swapped out our living room furniture at least twice since these people got theirs.

The girl offered me her hand. "I'm Heather's sister, Lane. Have we met?"

I worked hard not to stare, to behave normally. "No, but your sister's mentioned you." That she'd dated Aaron Robinson. Until last summer, when her friends spotted him at a party heading into a bedroom with another girl. A little too much of a coincidence for my taste.

Lane blinked a few times. "I'm sorry, I didn't catch your name."

"Oh, right. Skylar. Skylar Hoyt."

If possible, Lane's face lit up even more. "You sew with my sister, right? She's talked about you a lot. Says you're very talented." Her gaze whisked down and back up. "Which I can see."

I hadn't contributed a single stitch to my outfit but didn't bother correcting her.

"Everyone's hanging around in the kitchen." Lane led me through the entryway. She gestured to the living room crammed with empty seats. "I've got no idea why."

When I had a clear shot of the crowded kitchen, I wished Abbie hadn't felt so weird about bringing Owen. "All those women are going to ask me if I'm babysitting," Abbie had said. "And even if they act nice to my face, they'll talk about me behind my back. No thank you."

I should've worked harder to convince her. The only face I recognized was Heather's, and I didn't know how happy she'd be to see me. It'd been over a week since our fight, and we hadn't talked since.

Lane smiled. "I hardly know anybody either."

Had I spoken my thoughts out loud? But I guess staring blankly at the crowd probably made me pretty obvious.

"I've never been to a bridal shower," I said. "I didn't even know I was supposed to bring a gift until my mom told me this morning."

"She wouldn't have cared." Lane smiled at Heather, who nodded emphatically at something a gray-haired woman said. "My sister's basically the nicest person on the planet."

"I agree." But only if the tie went to Amy Ross.

"Are you in high school? College?"

"In between," I said. "I'm starting at Johnson County in August."

"Cool." She poured herself a cup of coffee. "You want one?"

"No thanks."

"There's sodas and stuff too. I wish Heather would start eating. I'm starving, but we're supposed to wait for her."

I helped myself to a Dr Pepper and tried to study Lane discreetly. I couldn't picture dark Aaron with light, airy Lane. Hadn't Heather said they dated a couple years? My mind filled with questions. *Was he nice to you? Did he push you to do things you didn't want to? Were you as hypnotized by his looks as I was, or were you smarter?*

I sipped my Dr Pepper. "So, where do you go to school?"

"I've been at KU, but I'm heading to Africa in a few weeks."

"Oh, that's right. Heather mentioned that to me. Are you nervous?"

Lane grinned. "Terrified. I've been once before, but to go for an entire year—"

"Hey, you made it!"

I looked up to see Heather weaving my direction. At the sight of her wide, genuine smile, relief flooded me.

She drew me close for a hug. "Where's Abbie?"

"Oh, she . . ." But I couldn't think of an excuse quick enough. "She felt weird about coming."

Heather's bright face flickered with a frown. "She shouldn't have. We'd have loved for her to come."

"I told her so."

"Come here." Heather gripped my arm. "I've got something to show you."

Lane groaned. "Please start eating. I'm starving."

Heather rolled her eyes good-naturedly, then turned toward the crowd of women. "Hey, gals? Gals?" Slowly everyone hushed. "I've got to run upstairs and show my friend Skylar something, so Lane's going to start the food, okay?"

Lane stuck out her tongue. "So not what I meant."

Heather stuck hers out as well, then pulled me through the living room. "Everyone's been asking to see it, but I wanted to show you first."

"Heather." I swallowed. "About some of the stuff I said last week—"

She waved away my words. "Forget it, Skylar. Really."

"Yeah?"

"Yeah." She jogged up the short flight of stairs to a hallway full of doors. "But that actually leads into what I wanted to show you." She opened the first door, and lying on the narrow bed was a dress bag.

Heather beamed. "I finished my dress."

"Oh, good," I said brightly. I didn't want her to know it crushed me that she'd done it without me. And that she'd made the wrong dress. One that said she hadn't forgiven herself for—

Heather yanked down the zipper, revealing the whitest dress I'd ever seen. Like the white of people's teeth on toothpaste commercials.

"It's perfect." I caressed the silk. "But—"

"But why did I change my mind?" Heather smiled. "You."

"Me?"

211

"Yeah. I started thinking about what you said, and you were just so . . . right. I mean, what a hypocrite I was being, right? I'm always telling you kids that nothing is too big, too dark, too shocking for Jesus, and then I held on to this horrible thing in my past." She hugged the dress to herself. "After you left that day, I prayed. And I could feel God saying to me that I was forgiven. That in his eyes, I'm just as pure as the day I was born. And the dress should be white to testify to that."

Tears streaked both our faces, but we smiled.

"I know we were going to make it together, but I needed to do this myself. I prayed with every stitch, and stopped to weep so many times . . . But here it is." Heather returned her dress to the bed, smoothing wrinkles in the fabric. "And I feel the most wonderful sense of . . . freedom."

I buried my face in my hands, sobbing, and sank to the floor.

"What is it?" Heather crouched beside me, her hand smoothing my hair like a mother's.

"Here I was telling you to forgive yourself"—I hiccupped—"yet I hadn't forgiven *myself.*"

"For what, sweetie?"

Laughter from downstairs bubbled up the hallway.

I swiped my hands across my cheeks, clearing away the tears and probably half my makeup. "Now's hardly the time and place."

Heather gripped my shoulders and looked me in the eyes. "Now is always the right time for forgiveness. Tell me what's going on."

So I took a deep breath and once again relived that horrible night.

"Oh my," Heather said for maybe the h
in the last ten minutes. "I just can't belie
gaze wandered to the closed bedroom door. "I won⌐
Lane has any idea."

"I can't believe I'm possibly the girl you told me about.
The girl who broke them up."

"That only makes me love you more. They needed to be
broken up. Obviously." She shook her head. "I never liked
Aaron, but I didn't think he'd do something like *that*. That's
just . . . despicable."

I thought of Connor's suggestion, that maybe Eli had
fudged the truth, but I didn't speak it. I liked blaming Aaron,
especially since Heather thought him a scumbag, whereas
Eli had been my friend for years.

Of course, just because blaming Aaron was easiest didn't
mean it was right.

"Do you think we could talk to Lane about this?" I asked,
clasping my hands so they'd stop trembling. "I want to
know more about who Aaron is."

She nodded. "After the shower."

"No way." Lane shook her head emphatically. "He wouldn't
do that."

Heather sighed, her patience sounding worn. "Lane, if
you'd just consider it for a second . . ." She trailed off as
Lane continued wagging her head.

"Look, I'll be the first one to admit Aaron's not perfect.
That he's far from perfect. But in the two years we dated,
he was totally respectful."

Heather narrowed her eyes. "*Totally* respectful?"

Lane shifted her weight. "Okay, maybe not *totally* respectful. But he understood what 'no' meant. For the most part." Lane looked at me. "I hope I'm not being insensitive. It sounds like you went through something awful. But I don't think Aaron would've done that."

Now two of the three people who'd heard my recollection of that night doubted it lined up with the truth.

"Although it wouldn't have been uncommon for Aaron to have drugs, would it?" Heather asked, her voice somehow gentle but pointed.

Lane shot her sister a look Abbie and I sometimes exchanged. A "how dare you go there" kind of look. "Being friends with Nate doesn't mean he was doing them. And this is too big an accusation to assume guilt by association." When Lane looked back at me, her expression and voice softened. "Is there no one else who could've done it?"

I shifted. "Not as easily as Aaron."

"Well . . ." Lane's jaw hardened and she shook her head. "No. The Aaron I know wouldn't have done that. You should consider who else might have."

25

I realized I'd been sitting there staring at my yellow polished cotton instead of pinning together the pieces that would become my dress for Heather's wedding. I reached for a straight pin and tried to keep my brain on task. Normally sewing absorbed all my attention. I'd start on a project, look up, and five hours would have slipped away. But ever since Saturday, since Lane defended her slimy ex-boyfriend, I couldn't think about anything else.

Again and again, I'd turned over the events of Jodi's party, hoping to find something. A hidden clue to unlock the truth of what had happened. Three days later, my efforts were still fruitless.

But right now I didn't need to think about that night, just this dress. Threading the pin through the fabric, watching the neckline come together.

"What's up?"

"Ouch!" I yelped as the pin pricked my tender fingertip.

Abbie grimaced. "Sorry. I assumed you'd heard me come in."

I sucked on my finger before the blood could stain my carefully selected fabric. "You need something?"

215

"I'm heading to class. Cool if I hand him off to you?" Without waiting for an answer—or for me to put away my straight pins—she dumped Owen onto my lap.

"Yeah, sure." I hastily pushed away sharp objects and arranged him better on my hip.

Abbie turned to leave, but paused when something caught her eye.

"Is this what you're making?" From my bed, she picked up the pattern envelope.

"Yeah. It's for Heather's wedding."

"Wow." She looked from the faded artist rendering to the pieces draped around my sewing machine. "It's adorable."

"Connor says I'll look like a 1950s housewife."

Abbie snorted. "What does he think you should wear to the wedding? Sweatpants?"

"I think he just wishes I'd dress a little more normal."

"But what's the fun in that? It's gonna be beautiful." Abbie returned the pattern to the bed. "You're really talented, you know."

She said that last part quietly. Abbie and I didn't compliment each other often. Except when forced, like if she said, "I look so fat," I'd obviously say, "No you don't. You look great." And vice versa.

"Too bad it's not something important." I packed away my materials as best I could with one hand.

"Who says it's not important?"

"You know what I mean."

She shook her head.

"It's not like nursing or teaching or something actually valuable to the world."

Abbie frowned. "If it wasn't valuable, why would God waste time giving you the talent?"

I stared at her. "I guess I never thought of God giving it to me."

"Of course he did. When Owen was born, Amy gave me a card that said every good thing comes from above." She tapped my sewing machine. "That includes this." She glanced at my alarm clock. "Okay, now I really need to go." Over her shoulder she called, "He'll be ready for his nap in forty-five minutes."

Then she dashed out the door and left me sitting there, caught totally off guard.

I closed my eyes and tried not to pay too much attention to their conversation. Tricky, since they kept asking my opinion.

"What do you think, Skylar?" Lisa popped her bubble gum. "The guy leaning against the fence. I say an eight."

Madison chewed on the stem of her sunglasses. "See, I think he's a six who acts like an eight."

"What do you think, Skylar?" Lisa asked again.

"I don't know."

"Oh, that's right," Lisa stage-whispered to Madison. "She's got a boyfriend now."

They giggled, and I bit back a frustrated growl. Why had I thought it'd be a good idea to come out with them? Guilt had made the decision for me. I'd been dodging their calls since I returned from Hawaii.

Hawaii. It seemed like a million years ago.

"Hello? Skylar?"

I blinked and realized one of them had said something to me. "What?"

"Eli's here." Madison nodded at the entrance.

I shifted at the sight of him swaggering into the fenced-off pool area. John trailed behind him, as always.

Madison nudged Lisa. "How would you rate John? A three? A two?"

Lisa rolled her big, clear eyes. "Are negative numbers allowed?"

Eli spotted me. Surprise crossed his face, but an instant later it vanished. He said something to John and they headed toward us. Toward the group of empty chaises next to me.

"Great," I muttered.

"You wanna go?" Madison asked.

"No." I straightened my back. "My family pays to belong here just like his."

As I watched Eli dodge a group of kids running around the pool, pride bloomed within me. The girl I'd been this spring would've tucked tail and run from what was sure to be a not-fun exchange, but now I found myself amused rather than nervous. Something to be thankful for. Something to smile about.

Eli, unfortunately, assumed I intended the smile for him and he smiled back. "What's going on, girl?" His voice sounded oddly casual.

"Sitting at the pool."

"Right." He plopped into the chaise beside me and made a show of looking around. "No bodyguard, I see."

"I gave him the day off."

On the other side of me, Lisa groaned. "You gotta be kidding me."

At first I thought she meant John, who was making a production out of taking off his shirt, but she appeared to be looking past him. Then I saw—Jodi and Alexis stood near the entrance, scouting out chairs.

I sat up straighter. "Unbelievable."

The seven of us hadn't all been together since sophomore year when the whole Alexis-Seth-Madison triangle exploded.

Alexis and Jodi spotted us at the same time. Alexis seemed intent on pulling Jodi off to another section of the pool, but Jodi squared her shoulders and marched our direction. Alexis dragged her feet like a moping toddler.

"Hey, guys," Jodi said, her smile bright like sunshine. "Guess we weren't the only ones who thought the weather was perfect for swimming."

It was ninety degrees outside and sticky as a cinnamon roll. The only other smart choice would be hitting the air-conditioned mall.

"Hey, Alexis," Madison said with a fake smile.

Alexis's delicate features hardened—her mouth pursed, her jaw set. She snagged the chaise beside John and made a show of dragging it several feet away.

Jodi glanced at her, then down the row at Lisa and Madison. They pointedly turned away from her. They probably thought it's what I'd want.

Jodi looked at me.

I'd sworn to myself that I'd loathe her for all eternity. I thought I'd doubt her sincerity to the very end. That I'd never be able to trust her, especially around Connor. But when her eyes met mine, searching, the fight drained from me. Jodi and I were on the same side. I was over it.

"I like your shirt," I said, and I did. "Where'd you get it?"

Alexis, Lisa, and Madison united—they all looked at me with wide eyes. Eli and John looked too, but only because I'd been the last one to speak. They never seemed in tune with whatever drama we girls had going on.

Jodi's face brightened as she took a seat on the other side of Alexis. "You're gonna hate it when I tell you."

"Seriously. Gap?"

"You know me. I own maybe two things from other stores."

I groaned. "That's just not right."

"I've worked there for two years and get a discount. What do you expect?"

"A little creativity."

"So not my thing."

Jodi smoothed sunscreen on her arms, then offered the bottle to Alexis, who whipped it from her hand like a little kid stealing back a favorite toy.

Jodi turned back to the rest of us. "Cool suit, Lisa."

"Thanks," Lisa said in a cautious voice. She glanced at me, seeming unsure of how to handle this. She didn't have anything personal against Jodi, but we'd spent a lot of time trash-talking her recently.

Madison stood and wrapped her long hair in a loopy bun. "It's too hot. I'm getting in." She surveyed the rest of us. "Anyone else?"

"Sure." I dropped my sunglasses to the ground.

"Yeah, me too," Lisa said.

"Of course." Alexis acted as though she didn't intend for us to hear, but obviously she *did* intend, because from three chaises down, I heard just fine.

I swiveled in my seat, facing her. "Do you have something to say, Alexis?"

She smiled sweetly. "I just think it's great how the three of you have formed, like, a little club. What do you guys call yourselves? The boyfriend stealers? The trampy—"

"I didn't steal anybody's boyfriend," Lisa said, standing. "*You* stole *mine*."

John sank lower in his lounge.

"Whatever. You guys were over. You just didn't want to admit it." Alexis glared at Madison. "Unlike me and Seth."

Madison laughed, big and careless. "Alexis, it was two years ago. Get over it." Then she took several steps toward the pool and slid into the cool water, effectively escaping the response Alexis stuttered.

Alexis squinted at Madison's slippery figure beneath the water. "I never liked her."

Lisa turned to me and said, "Let's just go. This isn't fun anymore."

"I'm not being chased out of my own pool," I said, gripping the hot concrete with my bare toes.

"You think everything belongs to you. Don't you, Skylar?" Alexis said. "You think you can do whatever you want and it doesn't affect anybody else. This is your world. The rest of us are just living in it."

"Don't talk to her like that." Eli's response sounded lazy, as if he hadn't intended to defend me, just reacted.

Alexis snapped upright in her chair. "*You* don't talk to me. Period. My boyfriend has a black eye thanks to you."

"Your boyfriend deserved it." Eli shielded his eyes and looked at Alexis. "I'd do it again in a heartbeat."

"Okay, Eli," I said in a threatening voice. I so didn't want to get into all that.

He answered with a wry laugh. "What's with you? It's like no matter what I do, it's wrong." His eyes, as blue as the pool I now stood beside, pierced me. "Tell me the truth. Did you ever actually like me, or did you just date me because of Aaron?"

"Because of Aaron?" Alexis's gaze flicked between the two of us. "Somebody explain."

I sighed. "Eli, I did like you. Okay?"

Madison bobbed up along the edge of the pool. She squinted up at Lisa and me. "You guys coming in, or what?"

"Somebody better tell me what's going on," Alexis shrieked. "Or I'm going to freak out."

"*Going* to?" Lisa said.

"You say you liked me, but you never acted like you did. Not for one second." Eli's voice rose with each word. "If I hadn't walked in and rescued you from Aaron, you'd never have given me a shot. Would you?"

Was it possible to hear blood racing through your veins? I kept my gaze locked on Eli, but I could feel the eyes of everyone else.

"What are you guys talking about?" Alexis asked. "What happened with Aaron?"

I thought of Connor, of how nicely he'd listened through the whole thing.

Of Heather.

Of Lane.

They'd all been practice. Practice for this moment, for these people. These were the ones who needed to hear what had happened to me that night. They'd been the closest to me—except Madison—and they'd witnessed my painful year of reinvention. They needed to know the story behind the story.

I'd gone all the way to Hawaii to try to escape this moment, and now I knew why. It was horrible.

I looked away from Eli, to the rest of my old friends, not quite sure where to begin.

"Tell us, Skylar." Alexis planted her hands on her narrow hips. "What happened?"

"At Jodi's party last year—"

"You don't have to do this, Skylar." Eli's eyes shone with regret. "You don't have to tell them."

Alexis roared at this. "I want a real explanation! I'm tired of being left in the dark!"

Quick like a Band-Aid. One, two, three . . .

"Aaron roofied me at Jodi's party. Nothing happened, but only because Eli caught him in time." I looked at Eli, who appeared miserable. "I'm grateful. That hasn't changed."

"Aaron wouldn't do that," Alexis said. "He's a nice guy. And the way he tells it—"

"Alexis, shut up," Lisa said. "Skylar just told us something huge. Can you think about someone other than yourself for five seconds?"

"Wait," I said. "How does Aaron tell it?"

Alexis blinked her long lashes at me. "He says you clearly had too much to drink and Eli's a jealous psycho. And that you left without even acknowledging him."

Eli sneered. "What'd he expect? He drugged her. I know it. His friends had the stuff."

I blinked at him. "His friends had the stuff? What does that mean?"

"I . . ." Eli glanced at our audience.

"Did you or did you not see Aaron put something in my drink?"

"Okay, so I didn't *exactly* see him put something in there, but—"

"What's wrong with you?" I marched back to my chair, snatched my shorts and tank, and wrestled them over my suit. "You said you saw him."

Eli swallowed hard. "I think what I said is that I *maybe* saw him."

"I don't care!" I poked him in the collarbone with my finger. "You told me you saw him, and I believed you."

He kept his gaze fixed on the ground. "I saw you and him talking, and then he went into the kitchen to get you a drink. Sarah Humphrey came over and handed him the cup that he gave to you."

I blinked rapidly. "So you didn't actually see a roofie."

"Well, not right then, but that thug boyfriend of Sarah's had them. John and I saw them earlier in the night. Remember?" Eli appealed to John, but he seemed unwilling to say anything. Eli swallowed again and looked at me. "We did. So, I mean, it's obvious that Aaron and Nate had worked out something, and Sarah was doing the legwork. It's obvious."

He turned to the rest of the group, as if waiting for them to agree. No one spoke.

"The only thing that's obvious"—I jammed my feet into my shoes, ready to march all the way home—"is that you were willing to do whatever it took to get me."

"How did you plan to get home?"

I turned. Jodi, Lisa, and Madison had followed me out to the parking lot.

"I hadn't really thought that far ahead."

"Let's take my car." Jodi fished keys from her pool bag. "And we better hurry. Only a matter of time before Eli comes out here after you."

We giggled as we sprinted toward her car. With my secret out, I felt light. So light that if a gust of wind came through, it might pick me up and carry me away.

"Where are we going?" I asked as we fussed with seat belts.

Jodi grinned and said, "Where do you think?"

"Sixth grade," Jodi said into her custard.

"*Sixth* grade?" I said. "How did I not know this?"

"Because that's not the worst of it." She bit her lip, trying not to smile. "Dylan Hollis."

"Dylan Hollis!" the three of us shrieked. Other patrons of Sheridan's turned and stared.

"No way," Madison said. "I mean, Dylan's so . . . Dylan. Especially in sixth grade. How did that ever happen?"

Jodi hid her red face in her hands, laughing. "We were on the yearbook team together because my mom thought I needed something brainier than cheerleading and—"

"Stop right there," Lisa said. "This is way too after-school-special. A beautiful, popular girl working late on yearbook with the class loser . . ."

"Forget Dylan Hollis. I can't get past the sixth grade part," I said. "It could've been Carter Shaw, and I'd feel just as horrified."

"Ooh, Carter Shaw," Jodi said. "Totally forgot about that guy."

"Yeah, whatever happened to him?" Lisa asked.

"I don't know who—" Madison stopped herself. "Oh, wait. Is he that guy who played on the guys' baseball team when we were freshmen? Dark hair, intense eyes?"

"That's the one." Jodi smiled at me. "Skylar and I liked him and both vowed we'd stay away."

"He was into you." I'd never admitted it before. "He had a thing for blondes."

"Like it matters anymore," Jodi said. But her face pinkened as she bit back a smile.

"It seems to be a common problem for you two," Madison said. "Liking the same guys, who like both of you back."

Jodi tilted her head at me, her smile cautious. "It's a miracle our friendship survived."

"Yeah." I tried to smile but couldn't. "Maybe you picked up on this at the pool, but I didn't mean to start dating Eli. The morning after, when he took me home, he kissed me, and . . . and after everything he'd just done for me . . ."

I thought of the hazy summer morning, of the clicking gas pump, of Eli inching closer and closer.

I looked Jodi in the eyes. "But I should've kept my promise to you."

She shrugged, looking weary. Of Eli? Of our battles? "It sounds like you might not have been thinking your clearest."

"Why didn't you tell us?" Lisa asked in a mouselike voice.

I blinked at her. I'd kinda forgotten Lisa's and Madison's presence. "I guess I was embarrassed to have put myself in that position. You know, I always tried to look like I had it all together, but that night . . ." I took a wobbly breath. "That night I so didn't."

Eli's words back at the pool haunted me: "It's obvious that Aaron and Nate had worked out something, and Sarah was doing the legwork. It's obvious."

But nothing about what happened to me seemed obvious anymore. Especially when it came to who could be trusted about the events at that party.

"What do you guys remember?" I asked. "I mean, do you think Eli's right? That Aaron and his friend had arranged everything?"

At first, none of them spoke.

"I wasn't there. I don't know," Madison said.

"I remember seeing you talk to Aaron, but not much else." Lisa shrugged, looking helpless. "I wasn't really paying attention."

I turned to Jodi, praying she held some nugget of information that would blow this whole thing open. Make it obvious who was to blame and who wasn't. And hopefully that information said "Aaron" in big, bold letters.

But Jodi shrugged as well. "I'm sorry. I hardly remember a thing about that night. I think I passed out even before you and Aaron went upstairs."

My hope dissolved, and I took a slow bite of my melting ice cream. "I guess I just need to get over it. And I can do that. I mean, so what if I never know what really happened?"

"Don't say that," Madison said. "That sucks."

I smiled at her. "I agree, but—" Was that . . . ? Yep. Eli marched our direction. "We should've gone to a different one."

They turned to see.

Jodi started to get to her feet. "I'll get rid of him, Skylar."

"No, it's okay." I stood, which made Eli slow his steps. "This is mine to deal with."

As I walked toward him, a whole spiel ran through my mind—about how I appreciated him following me up to that room regardless of what Aaron might or might not have done, how I never would've had the life I did now if he hadn't acted like he did, that I wouldn't want things to be any different—but Eli spoke first. "I'm gonna find out what happened."

I blinked at this, my rehearsed speech evaporating. "What?"

"That night. I'm gonna find out what happened. If Aaron drugged you or"—he swallowed—"not."

"Eli . . ." Thirty seconds ago I'd said it didn't matter, but the thought of knowing the truth made my heart beat a little faster. "You don't have to. I'm happy now, and—"

"I owe you." He stuffed his hands in the pockets of his swim trunks. "And I think you deserve to know."

That brought tears to my eyes. I looked away, at the passing traffic. "I'm sorry about this spring. I didn't mean to lead you on when—"

"I always knew you were in love with him. I don't know *why*, but that doesn't matter. If he makes you happy, then . . ." He shrugged. "You know. Whatever."

My phone sang to me from my back pocket. "That's probably him now," I said as I fished for it.

Nope—my house.

"Skylar." Mom sounded breathless. "I need you to come home right away. There's been—"

"Mom?" I said as she dissolved into tears.

"Just come home, okay?"

And then the line went dead.

26

Barely twenty-four hours later, Mom's and my plane touched down in Lihue. Mostly tourists occupied our connecting flight from Honolulu. A few residents dotted the crowd, but the air buzzed with vacation chatter. My ears snatched bits of conversation as we exited—hiking Na Pali and surfing lessons at Poipu Beach. A far cry from what I'd be doing on this trip—burying my grandfather.

"You double-checked that it's yours?" Mom asked as I pulled my suitcase off the carousel.

I nodded, and we headed into the fresh, sweet-smelling afternoon.

We didn't talk again until pulling onto Kapule Highway in our squatty rental car. "You doing okay?" I asked Mom, observing the slack of her face. I couldn't see her left eye anymore, but on the plane it'd twitched.

She exhaled a shaky breath. "I don't know."

I had no response for that. Maybe my father would've known what to say. I assumed she'd have preferred having him here instead of me, although she'd told him over and over that it was fine.

"There's no way you can go," she'd insisted last night as she stabbed at her salad but didn't eat a bite. "Not only are you breaking ground on the AMC project, you've got *two* meetings with prospective clients. No way."

"You come first, Teri."

It warmed me to hear him say it, and I wondered if it did her too.

"I know that," she said very quietly. "And that's why it's fine if you stay. Skylar and I will be fine."

And now I wondered if she'd been right. If only Abbie could've come too. It was totally impractical with summer school and Owen, but I sure missed her ability to fill up a silence.

"My father and I never got along well." It startled me to hear Mom's voice. "I assume you know that."

I shrugged.

Mom looked at me, then turned her attention back to the road. "I never thought we'd be back so soon."

"Do you miss it at all?"

She chewed on her lip as she thought. I'd never noticed her doing that before. I did the same thing sometimes. Used to be I'd have been horrified to recognize myself in her, but now it made me smile.

"Sometimes. In the winter, I guess I do. I've never cared for the cold." Mom frowned. "But I guess life's like that."

She left me to draw my own conclusions. "Cold?"

Mom smiled. "No. Like in the winter months—or in the times of trial and frustration—it's easy to long for happier times. When you think back on how it used to be, you only recall the good stuff. Like pineapple and sunshine and the feel of the ocean. But then you go back, and you're like, oh yeah, there's lots of bugs. And the bread mildews on the grocery store shelves. And it costs a fortune to live here."

She sighed. "Sorry. I bet none of that made any sense. I didn't sleep much last night."

"You're making sense." I thought of the spring, when I'd ached so badly from Connor's betrayal. At the time, all I'd remembered from my old life was the carefree fun, and how I'd never been hurt like he'd hurt me. I'd fallen back into being the old Skylar, only to rediscover the morning-after headaches and regrets. The dissatisfaction of it all.

Reinvention hurt, but at least it was a satisfying kind of pain. Like when you exercise.

I looked out the window at the palm trees and azure expanse of water. Strange to think how if I'd stayed, I might have been here for Papa's heart attack. My throat closed at the memory of him on the porch, wearing one of his ugly, old-man shirts, his fingers busy with his electronic poker game.

Something brushed against my leg. I turned to find Mom's hand, smooth and soft, patting me. A rare display of affection, and one I needed.

"I'm really proud of you," Mom said, her voice tight. "I know it's been a rough year and we've had our fair share of disagreements, but I see a lot of changes in you." She squeezed my leg, then withdrew her hand. "You're inspiring."

I closed my eyes, holding back tears. To hear her say that, I'd have redone this year a thousand times more.

"Grammy's told me over and over that the doctors said it was quick, virtually pain free," I said to Connor. "So that's good."

"It's great. I mean, as great as him dying could be, you know."

"I know." I tucked my legs underneath me. Not so long ago—but also very long ago—Papa and I had had a very important talk on this bench.

"How's your mom?"

"She's . . ." I glanced through the lit window. Mom sat at the so-old-it-was-back-in-again Formica table with a checkbook register and a box of something that looked like receipts. "She's surprisingly strong. I'm used to seeing my dad take care of everything important and my mom just decorating. It's strange to see her doing everyday stuff. Earlier she was scrubbing the toilet."

"That thought just doesn't compute."

"I know. I guess . . ." I caught myself biting my lip and smiled. "I guess she's why I've hesitated to go into design. I want to do something that matters, and I don't know how fashion can do that."

"But who says it's gotta be your work that makes you matter?" Connor said. "Think about everyone you've influenced this year. I mean, look at Jodi."

I ran my hands through my hair. "She's the real deal, isn't she?"

"All except the tan."

I giggled. "Connor, that's not nice."

"I'd say it to her face too."

I sighed. "Yeah, I know. That doesn't mean you should."

Across the street, at the tiny house Justin and Chase shared, the door opened. Justin stepped out, his eyes on me and his feet moving my direction.

"Hey, I see Justin and need to talk to him, okay?"

"The guy across the street? Who your grandma wanted you engaged to by now?" I heard him frowning.

"You want me to put you on speaker or anything?" I teased.

"No, just call me back later. And don't forget to mention me. And that I've been working out."

I grinned. "Call you later." I tucked my phone in my pocket and met Justin in the scabby yard. "Hi."

"Hi." He tugged at his shirt collar. "Sorry about your grandpa."

I nodded. "Thanks."

Justin cleared his throat. "I meant to call you after you left. I knew I should, but I couldn't really think of what to say. And then more and more time went by and . . ."

"It's fine."

"No it's not. I was really mean to you, Skylar—"

"Please don't apologize." I wrung my hands. "What you said to me, it was true. And it's what I needed to hear. To force me to go back home and do what I needed to do."

He frowned. "I'm glad it worked out okay. I think I've partially felt so bad because I was being really hypocritical. I accused you of using me to get over someone else, and I think I was using you too. To get over Janette. Remember the girl I told you about?"

Not by name. "Kinda."

"Well, I think I was just brokenhearted and wanted to move on. Right away. Regardless of what God had planned, or . . ." His eyes searched mine. "Or what it could've done to you."

"It's okay," I said as the door to Grammy and Papa's—or just Grammy's—house opened.

Light spilled onto the lawn, then darkened with Mom's silhouette. "Skylar?"

"Yeah, Mom?"

She stepped onto the porch. "Oh, hi, Justin."

"Hi, Mrs. Hoyt. Sorry about your dad."

"Thank you." She pulled the door closed behind her with a soft click. "Mom said you stayed with her until the medical examiner came and went. That was very nice of you."

Justin shrugged. "She's been really great to me since I moved in. Both of them were. It was the least I could do."

One of those strange silences settled over us, where no one has anything else to say, yet no one knew how to leave.

"I should get back inside." Mom glanced at me. "Take your time."

I took a step toward the house. "I was getting ready to come in anyway."

"See you at the funeral," Justin said. "Let me know if there's anything else I can do."

I smiled. "Thanks."

As we headed our different directions, Mom said to me, "He's a nice young man."

"Yeah, he is."

"You break his heart?"

I laughed a little. "He somehow survived."

Mom touched my shoulder as I reached for the doorknob. "You mind if we sit outside for a couple minutes and talk? I convinced Grammy to go take a bath."

"Yeah, sure."

She settled onto the porch bench, and I followed her lead.

"I want to talk to you about your father and me."

My heart seemed to pause, then raced. "Are you getting divorced?"

Her jaw clenched and she shook her head. "Never. I understand why you'd think that, though. Your father and I have had . . . well, not an easy go of it for the last couple years."

Talk about an understatement.

"We both accept the blame for this, but I give your dad all the credit for us being back on track now. After Abbie had Owen . . ." Mom stared out into the night for a second, then continued. "After Abbie had Owen, your father and I decided to stay together. Mostly for Abbie—for all three of you, really. We went to counseling. We didn't have any crazy blowups at each other. And I really thought that was enough."

She turned to me, eyes shimmery with tears. "Even though we decided to stay together, in my heart I never made another commitment to *love* your father. To cherish him. In sickness and health, in good times and bad. I was just going through the motions of being married. I thought that was enough."

Mom sighed. "When you wanted to come to Hawaii and we decided to take a family vacation, I was elated. Even though I'd decided to stay in Kansas City, I harbored regret for not getting to live where I wanted. But our time in Hawaii changed everything. We'd been here barely twenty-four hours when I realized I didn't want to stay. This isn't my home anymore. My home is with your dad, with you and Abbie, with Owen." Tears spilled down her cheeks as she caressed my hair, pushing it behind my ears. "And I'm so, so sorry for all the things I did that made you doubt I want you."

We moved toward each other, hugging and crying.

"It's okay, Mom," I said into her hair. "It's done. It's over."

She cried harder, and I understood. Sometimes you've been gripping that pain, that shame, for so long it took a long time to cry it all out.

"Mom."

She pulled back and looked at me.

I took a deep breath. "I don't know if now's the best time. But there's something I've been hiding from you and Dad. Something I need to tell you. See, about a year ago, I was at this party . . ."

27

I'd been to two funerals before, Grandma Hoyt's and Grandpa Hoyt's. For Grandma's I was seven, for Grandpa's seven and a half. I'd worn the same black velvet dress to both funerals, the same itchy wool tights, and the same shiny shoes that were a touch too small even at the first one. Almost the entire town had shown up at the First Baptist Church of Medicine Lodge, Kansas. They'd dressed in dark clothes, donned somber faces, and hugged me close as if they'd known me.

Papa's funeral was different altogether. Grammy, Mom, and I wore matching flowing muumuus (which, thankfully, no one documented with pictures). We sat in the front row of the church, our necks decorated with leis of sweet-smelling plumeria. The other women present wore traditional Hawaiian dresses, and the men wore aloha shirts untucked over their slacks. Not a shade of black, or even gray, could be found in the whole church.

Others who'd known Papa much better than I had, and much better than Mom had, went to the stage to speak of him. They spoke of his service in rebuilding Kapaa after Iniki, of how he took time to talk to new people at church, and of how he loved his family, especially his girls. That sent Mom into hysterical sobs.

Even in June, she and Papa had barely spoken to each other. I knew from my conversation with him that he'd loved her, just didn't know how to say it. So that morning, as we'd prepared food for the after-service feast, I'd told her all he'd said to me.

Tears had pricked her eyes, and she took several deep breaths before speaking. "I don't want it to be like that with you and me. I want to say nice things when I can, when it matters."

"Me too," I said. "Your hair is pretty."

Mom's frown morphed into a smile. "I like your earrings."

"You have very straight teeth."

This made her giggle—she sounded like Abbie. She returned to chopping fresh fruit. "I know you've heard my parents, especially Grammy, indirectly say a lot of things about you. About how I screwed up my life by getting married so young, how I disappointed them." She put down the knife and looked at me. "You've never been a disappointment."

I hugged her, not wanting to risk her seeing my relief. I thought it'd hurt her feelings if she knew I'd been carrying around that fear with me since last winter, when we met in Starbucks and she told me about my conception. How I'd trapped her in a life she wasn't sure she wanted.

And now, as we sat through Papa's memorial service in our matching muumuus and leis, my mind replayed the words over and over. *You've never been a disappointment, never been a disappointment.* I wished Papa had thought to tell my mom the same thing before it was too late.

Of course, maybe because he didn't, my mom knew she should.

For five days, Mom sat with Grammy as she cried. She held Grammy's hands, wrinkled and thin-skinned like tissue paper used over and over, and let her sob about what a wonderful man Kelani had been. About how much fun they'd always had together. About how her girlfriends were so jealous when she'd snagged him. She said more nice things about him in five minutes than I'd heard her say in our two weeks back in June.

When I rolled my suitcase out to the living room, Grammy burst into a fresh batch of tears. "I can't believe you're leaving me already."

"Oh, Mom." My mom sank onto the couch. "Are you sure you don't want to come back to Kansas City with us? We can call and get you a ticket right now. It's no problem."

Grammy wiped her eyes. "I don't like the cold."

"It's July, Mom."

"But it'll get cold."

"Not until October."

"I couldn't leave your father. Not yet." She wiped her eyes again. "And Sylvie and the kids will be here this evening. They're staying a full week."

My aunt Sylvie and her family had been in the middle of a European vacation when the call came about Papa. No one told me if they'd been unwilling to leave, or if it just hadn't been practical.

Mom ignored the snub about the length of our stay.

"Well, if after they leave you don't want to be alone, you'd be welcome at our house."

"I'll be fine." Grammy smoothed nonexistent wrinkles from her skirt. "There's lots to do. Cleaning and putting things in order. You know."

"But none of it needs doing right away," Mom said, something she'd repeated several times during our stay. "Why not go to the mainland with us, and then come back when it's less painful?"

Grammy set her jaw. "It'll always be painful. I spent fifty-four years of my life with your father."

"That's not how I meant it, Mom. I just meant when the pain isn't as fresh. When you can think clearer."

"I can think just fine," Grammy snapped. Then she rubbed her eyes, which drooped from sleepless nights. "I'm sorry, Teri. I'm just on edge right now."

"It's fine." Mom reached for Grammy's hand. "I want to do whatever I can to make this easier for you."

Grammy gazed at my mom, her eyes seeming old and wise. "Sorry, baby girl. This is something I have to go through by myself. But the Lord will see me through. He always does."

My mom nodded and squeezed Grammy's hand. She looked at me. "It's time?"

I nodded.

"Don't worry about me." Grammy stood. "I'll barely be alone four hours."

I kissed her round cheek. "I love you, Grammy."

She drew me near. "And I love you, my little Skylark." She pulled my mom close as well. "And you too."

In the car, as we drove down the poorly paved road, Mom

released a shaky sigh. "I wish Sylvie and them hadn't missed their connection. I feel horrible about leaving her alone."

"You think Grammy will change her mind? About coming to Kansas City, I mean?"

Mom shook her head. "I doubt it. She'll want to deal with her grief all on her own." She sighed again. "It's the Ka'aihue way."

Hours later, I awoke in my bedroom to the sight of Abbie's beaming face.

"Hi," I said in a hoarse voice.

"I thought you'd never wake up."

I pressed a hand to my head and blinked a couple times in the brilliant sunlight my curtains couldn't seem to keep out. I felt fuzzy and disconnected, same as I had the last time we'd taken the red-eye out of Hawaii.

Abbie plopped onto my bed. "I've got something exciting to tell you. Owen slept through the night."

"Great," I said through a yawn.

She gave me a look. "Nice enthusiasm."

"Sorry, I'm just . . ." I yawned again. "Sleepy."

Abbie laughed. "Believe me, I know the feeling." She fussed with the ragged hem of her shorts. "So I've got something else to tell you too. You know Dr. Prentice?"

"Mom and Dad's counselor?"

"Yeah. Well, she's sorta my counselor now too."

I blinked a couple times, waiting for an intelligent response to come to mind. "I don't understand."

She took a deep breath. "I'd been talking to Amy a lot." She hesitated. "Ross."

"I know who Amy is."

"Okay, you were just giving me a blank look."

"Hello? I just woke up after four hours of sleep."

"Sorry, sorry. Anyway, I've been talking to Amy, just about how I've been feeling isolated and overwhelmed and depressed and a whole myriad of horrible adjectives. And then I started having these thoughts. About how maybe I made the wrong decision about keeping Owen, but then I'd be with him and I'd think, how could I have ever thought about giving him up? I must be a horrible mother."

I floundered for her hand and found it on her lap. "You're a great mother."

Abbie smiled. "Amy said I should talk to Mom and Dad about seeing a counselor. I'd thought about it before, but I guess I didn't want to admit I was having such a rough time. Amy said transitioning to motherhood even in the best circumstances is hard and that I shouldn't be embarrassed. But I still was. I talked to Dad about it while you guys were gone, and he took me to Dr. Prentice. I've only gone once, but I just feel so much . . . freer."

What kind of big sister was I? "I'm so sorry I had no idea how you were feeling."

She shook her head, silencing me. "I didn't want you knowing. You do everything so perfectly—"

I snorted.

"—that I didn't want to tell you. But I should have."

I squeezed her hand. "You've got to stop punishing yourself for what happened. And I can say that to you only because I've just recently worked through that myself. Just because you've got Owen doesn't mean you have to hide out at the house all the time."

Abbie bit her lower lip. "Yesterday I was taking Owen for a walk and went by Jenna's house. It was her birthday, and I just knew . . ." Her eyelashes fluttered as she battled tears. "Sure enough. The street was full of cars. She was my best friend."

"I'm so sorry."

Abbie lay on the bed and nestled into my pillow. "I understand that it's weird. I mean, I get why she's not talking to me anymore and why Chris broke up with me. I just hope if I were in their situation, I'd be a little more understanding."

"Well, I think it's great that you're in counseling. And it's good for Owen too."

Abbie's eyes looked heavy despite her full night of sleep. "Thanks for understanding. For not thinking I'm just being dramatic."

"You? Never."

She smiled at me. "And thanks for putting up with me these last couple months. I know I've been a little . . . fussy."

I grinned. "I don't know if 'fussy' is the best word. But you're welcome."

Her eyes closed. "Your bed is comfy." She'd barely gotten out the words when her breathing deepened and her face went slack.

I closed my eyes too, grateful to return to sleep. And grateful for my sister, and how strong she was, whether she knew it or not.

28

"Wow," Connor said as I walked across Loose Park. "You look . . . Wow."

I grinned. "Not too 1950s?"

"No, just perfect." He took my hand and spun me around once. "I can't believe you made this. It looks like something you could've bought. Only better."

I glanced at the crowd gathered in the rose garden. The park looked beautiful, full of white wooden chairs draped with violet tulle. "Where's your family?"

Connor tugged me closer, where my view wasn't obstructed, and pointed. They'd already been seated and chatted with another family I didn't recognize.

Connor glanced behind me. "Abbie couldn't make it?"

I shook my head. "Owen woke up from his last nap with a fever and a nasty cough. She's at some after-hours pediatrician place now."

"Is it serious?"

"My mom thinks it's just some bug he picked up at playgroup or something, but Abbie insisted on taking him. Are Jodi or Eli here yet?" The rose garden, while big, didn't allow for much parking. Heather and Brent had been forced to pare down the invite list, but still our entire youth group had been invited.

"Not yet." Connor eyed me carefully. "You want to save them seats?"

"Sure."

"Really?"

I shrugged. "I think Jodi and I are on our way to being friends again."

An usher approached me. "Bride or groom's side, miss?"

"I've got this one." Connor offered me his arm. "She's all mine."

"There was a wreck on Ward Parkway," Jodi muttered as she slid into the seat beside me. Eli took the empty spot on the other side of Connor. "They've got it down to one lane and we were all just crawling." She looked forward at Heather and Brent, who stood with joined hands and shining faces. "What'd I miss?"

"Not much," I said. "Heather walked down the aisle. Pastor Greg's said lots of stuff about commitment and love."

"The flower girl picked her nose," Connor added.

Jodi made a face. "That's so gross." She assessed Heather. "Killer dress, by the way. You two did a great job."

I smiled. "It was all Heather. I just picked the color."

Jodi snickered as if I'd joked. It pleased me to think that my zeal for fashion, for the appropriate dress for Heather's big day, had impacted her life, had brought about change. Connor had been right to say I didn't need to define myself by what I did for a living, but that didn't mean God couldn't use my talent at all.

"Hey." Jodi nudged me, her tone different now. "Isn't that . . . ?"

I followed her gaze across the aisle, to the groom's side, where I recognized no one. "Who?"

"Lean this way." Jodi pushed me forward a little bit, and that's when I saw him—Aaron.

"Oh my gosh." My right hand gripped hers and my left hand Connor's.

"Ouch. What's going on?" Connor asked. Both he and Eli gave me curious looks.

"Aaron's here," Jodi said.

Connor squeezed my hand. "You want to leave?"

"No. This is good," I said, to remind myself. "Maybe now we can settle this thing."

"Maybe he's not coming," I said.

The four of us had been sitting at our table at the reception watching the door for Aaron's arrival. So far nothing.

"I'm sure he's coming. The reception is the only good part of a wedding," Connor said.

Jodi gave him a look. "Very romantic."

Eli wrung a cocktail napkin. "I don't think you should talk to him. Let Connor and me handle it."

"No," I said flatly. "I need to do this. I'm just going to ask him about that night. About his side of the story."

Eli snorted. "Like he'll tell the truth."

"Worst case, I won't know any more than I know now." I gulped, thinking of those dark, blank spaces between memories of Jodi's party. "And maybe that's okay."

247

But when something altered the course of your life as severely as that night had mine, you wanted every detail. You wanted to be able to hold it, turn it over, and inspect it. I had the fruit from that night—this new girl I'd become, Connor, new relationships with my family. That could be enough for me, but I wanted to know.

"There he is," the three of them said in unison.

Aaron loosened his tie and glanced around. Looking for Lane? I bet it hadn't crossed his mind that I'd be there. I doubted I ever crossed his mind at all. He touched the arm of the middle-aged woman he'd entered with—his mom?—and motioned to the bar. Shocking.

I pushed back my chair. "Be right back."

"Be careful," Connor said as Eli said, "Don't leave our sight."

They looked at each other and Eli nodded slightly, as if relinquishing responsibility. Then Connor said, "Just do whatever you have to do."

"And if he tries anything, kick him in the—"

"She's got it under control, guys," Jodi said, cutting off Eli.

I squeezed Connor's hand and marched away on my mission.

By the time I reached the bar, my head ached from grinding my teeth, and I thought everyone in the room must be able to hear the pounding of my heart.

I reached to tap him on the shoulder, my cold, clammy hand pausing midway, then finally making contact. I retracted it as quickly as I could.

Aaron smiled at me, looking a little surprised, a little wary. His bruise had healed since I last saw him almost a month before. "Oh, hey. It's you. Do you know Brent somehow?"

"Heather," I managed.

"Huh. Small world, I guess."

The bartender handed Aaron what looked like a glass of soda and another glass of something clear and fizzy. Then he gave me an inquisitive glance. "For you, miss?"

"Dr Pepper."

"I gotta get this to my mom." Aaron nodded the other direction. "Maybe I'll see you a little later."

He retreated a few steps.

I swallowed, then blurted, "I want to know what happened that night."

He froze and turned to me. "What night?"

I choked on the oatmeal-like lumps that kept forming in my throat. "At Jodi's party."

"Whose?"

"The one where we met. The one where—" Another lump that refused to go down.

Aaron glanced at the bartender, who fussed with the ice and various cans of soda, as if not wanting to hear our conversation. Heck, *I* didn't want to hear our conversation.

"Let me give this to my mother." Aaron's voice sounded spookily even. "Meet me outside the ballroom and we'll talk."

I nodded, then watched him walk away.

The bartender cleared his throat. "Your drink."

"Thank you." My hands shook as I reached for it. "Sorry you had to hear that."

"I've heard much worse in my profession." He nodded

in the direction Aaron had retreated. "Don't let him get away with a thing."

I dropped a dollar in the tip jar, then moved one foot in front of the other back to my table.

"What's going on?" Connor asked.

I handed him my drink but kept walking toward the doorway, where Aaron waited.

"Where are you going?" Eli asked, but I ignored him.

I made a conscious effort to keep my back straight, my head held high, as I neared Aaron. No matter what this conversation revealed, I wouldn't allow him to make me feel defeated. I'd been forgiven, and nothing could take that away from me.

Aaron smoothed his curls off his forehead as we walked the long corridor of the Sheraton, away from the reception hall and bustle of the other guests. "So what's the deal?"

I stopped and crossed my arms. "Did you roofie my drink?"

His jaw dropped. I didn't know that actually happened outside of cartoons. "Did I *what*?"

"You heard me," I said. "My drink was doctored at that party, and you did it."

"No I didn't. I'd have never done something like that."

"Oh yeah? It's not like you had a moral issue with taking me up to the Starrs' guest bedroom."

His face turned to stone. "You didn't seem to have any problem going up there with me."

"I was drugged! You think I'd go up to a bedroom with some guy I'd just met? I'd *never* have agreed to that."

He shrugged. "Alexis says your sixteen-year-old sister

just had a baby, so maybe being loose is a family trait or something."

Through gritted teeth, I said, "Don't you *dare* mention my little sister ever again."

Aaron shrugged and fixed me with a hard look. Apparently being accused of attempted rape didn't settle well with him.

"I was drugged," I insisted, remembering how the room had gone fuzzy, how my mouth felt full of sand, how my head burned the next morning. It'd been different from other headaches.

"Well, not by me. Maybe by that psychotic blond guy who attacked me a few weeks ago. Roofies seem like something that'd be up his alley."

I stamped my foot. "Why would Eli roofie me and then give *you* a black eye?"

"Maybe to make it look like he didn't." Aaron shrugged again. Careless. Annoying.

"You listen to me." When I came at him, he scrambled backward and pressed against the wall. "You've got no idea what that night did to me. What it cost me. *No* idea."

Aaron slinked to the right, creating space between us. "God knows what you've built that night into, but I don't know how else to tell you that you've got the wrong guy. I didn't put anything in your drink."

His first words echoed in my ear—"God knows."

God knew how I'd ached. God knew how I'd both appreciated everything that night gave me—him, inner strength, relationships—and yet sobbed for what it stole. Safety. Trust.

Aaron didn't know. I could never change that. No matter

how long I held him hostage out here, he wouldn't understand, but God still would. God knew what had happened that night, and that would have to be enough.

"Your friends had roofies that night, didn't they?" The question bubbled out of me before I could stop it. My voice sounded different, gentler, even though my insides were still tumultuous.

Aaron blinked, probably confused by the transformation. "I don't know. I don't, like, track their every move or anything."

"My friend saw them with roofies. He said Sarah's boyfriend—Nate, I think—had them."

Aaron shrugged yet again. Did he ever express himself any other way? "It's possible. So Nate had them. What does that have to do with me? I mean, maybe your friend saw them because he was buying them. Ever think of that?"

I shook the question away. It couldn't be Eli. It just couldn't. But if it wasn't Eli, and Aaron was being honest, who did that leave?

I squeezed my eyes shut and tried to walk through those early moments with Aaron. When he'd left to get me a drink, Jodi came to talk to me. She looked over at Aaron and said—

I snapped my eyes open. "You were talking to Sarah Humphrey. In the kitchen. When you were getting my drink."

"Maybe. I don't know."

"No, I saw you."

"I talk to Sarah a lot. She's Nate's girl."

"Did she give you the roofie?"

Aaron sighed. "No, okay? I've told you, like, a thousand times I've got nothing to do with this."

"Do you remember *anything* you talked about with her that night?" I could hear the desperation in my voice. I wanted answers so badly.

"I go to lots of parties, okay? I don't remember a specific one from a whole year ago." He looked ready to return to the reception, but I got in his way. I couldn't give up yet.

"Do you remember why you were there?" I asked. "Sarah and my friend don't get along." I remembered what Jodi had said to me that day at Panera when we ran into Sarah. "Jodi heard Sarah came just to get back at her, but nothing happened."

Something seemed to click in Aaron's mind. "*That* party . . ." He loosened his tie again. "Yeah, I remember now. After you made your dramatic exit, I went downstairs and all my friends had bailed."

"Was Sarah getting back at me too?" I asked, thinking of how I'd handed Jodi the scissors. How over the last couple years, Sarah's angry glare went first to Jodi and then skittered to me. "Is that why she helped you drug me?"

"For the last time, I didn't drug you." Aaron's hand ran through his hair. "Okay, that night . . . that night . . . you said you wanted a drink, so I went to get you one. Right?"

I nodded.

"When I went to get you a drink, Sarah came to talk to me. And . . ." He blinked at me several times. "What's your friend's name?"

"Jodi."

"Jodi," Aaron repeated. "I think that's right. Okay, I remember what happened. Sarah gave me a cup. She said it was Jodi's and asked me to give it to her. That's it. That's all that happened."

I leaned against the wall as the pieces came together. Sarah watching for the perfect opportunity to pay us back, like she'd come there to do. Then fleeing the scene before anything unfolded.

"Did she ever touch my cup?"

Aaron blinked. "What?"

"My cup! Did she ever touch my cup?"

He blinked even more. "I don't know. I maybe handed it to her for a second while I refilled mine, but—"

"Did Sarah ever say anything to you about Jodi and me? About"—I swallowed—"getting her hair cut off at a party?"

His eyes narrowed. "That was you?"

I nodded. "And she got us back, didn't she? She encouraged you to come talk to me, and then she fixed up our drinks when you weren't paying attention."

"I . . ." Aaron swallowed. "I mean, Sarah's got kind of a vengeful streak. I guess I wouldn't be surprised to hear she'd done something like that, but I never *saw* anything."

I took a deep breath and leaned against the wall. "You can go now."

He lingered. "Look, you're not gonna press charges or—"

"Just go away!"

He hesitated only a second longer, then scurried back to the reception.

I closed my eyes and slid along the wall to the ground. What did I do with this now? Did it mean anything? So Aaron hadn't drugged me. So what? He hadn't felt reservations about taking me upstairs. And he still might have done something had Eli not interrupted.

And what about Jodi? She'd said at Sheridan's that she

passed out before Aaron and I even went upstairs. What had happened to her when I wasn't watching?

"What happened?"

I opened my eyes to find Connor squatting on the floor in front of me. Eli and Jodi hovered behind him. All three watched with big, concerned eyes.

I released a shaky breath. "Aaron says he didn't do it. And from what he said, I think . . ." I looked at Jodi. "I think it was Sarah. I think she put something in both our drinks."

Jodi's eyes grew wider and her legs trembled. She sat, her raspberry-colored dress flaring around her. "Of course. That makes so much sense. All year Sarah kept saying this really weird stuff to me. *Strange* stuff, like . . . well, I shouldn't repeat it now that I'm a Christian. But . . ." She grabbed my hands. "Oh, Skylar, I'm so sorry. It's all my fault this happened to you. If I hadn't been so set on revenge with her, this never would've happened, and—" Jodi dissolved into tears and I hugged her close.

"Don't worry about me," I said. "I'm okay. I'm worried about *you*. About what might have happened."

She pulled away, shaking her head. "Nothing happened. I woke up in my room the morning after."

"How did you get up there?"

When she didn't answer right away, I swallowed hard. Jodi blinked rapidly. "I don't know."

Eli cleared his throat. "I carried you up there."

We turned to him and his face reddened. "I thought you'd just drunk too much. I didn't want to leave you in the living room, so . . ." He shrugged, then looked at me. "That's when I found you and Aaron. I heard you crying."

Jodi pressed trembling fingers to her mouth. "And that's

my fault." She turned her big, teary eyes to me. "Oh, Skylar, if only I hadn't done that thing to Sarah. If only I'd let those rumors about her and Trent slide, then she wouldn't have retaliated and—"

"And nothing would have changed," I said. "None of this would've happened. None of the good stuff."

Jodi bit her lower lip. "I keep picturing all these things that could've happened to you—"

"But they didn't. I'm fine, Jodi. *We're* fine."

She knit her fingers in her lap. "I'll never be able to forgive myself for this. For what I caused."

"You will," I said, "because I've finally forgiven myself for what happened. I'm 100 percent, truly, totally over it."

29

Pastor Greg smiled at the few of us seated in the sanctuary. "We're gathered here today because Teri and Paul Hoyt have requested to renew their wedding vows in front of their family and close friends."

Mom looked away from Greg for a second to wink at me. I winked back.

"It'll be a simple service," Mom had said back in August when she and Dad told Abbie and me. "Dr. Prentice thinks it's a good idea. It'll be just you girls, Grammy, and the Rosses. We'll all have dinner together afterward. Very casual, very low-key. Just a . . ."

"A celebration," Dad finished for her.

"Right." Mom smiled. "Of our renewed commitment to each other."

"Right," Dad said, and they beamed at each other like newlyweds. Which would have gagged me had I not felt so relieved.

And now a month later, Connor's fingers entwined with mine as we watched Mom and Dad take communion together.

My cell buzzed on my lap. "It's from Jodi," I whispered to Connor. It read, *What am I missing?* I grinned and tucked my phone away. There'd be time later to text her back.

Jodi had been at Vanderbilt for a few weeks, and it sounded like she'd settled in okay. She liked her room-mate and she'd already been asked out a couple times. Typical Jodi. Something I couldn't say about her too often anymore.

"Paul Hoyt, do you agree to renew your commitment to love and cherish Teri . . ."

I smiled as Greg read the traditional vows, the same ones my parents had pledged to each other almost twenty years ago. A wedding where I'd also been present. Although to this one they'd invited me.

We cheered loudly when Greg presented my newly recommitted parents. Until Dad drew Mom into a long kiss, then Abbie and I both groaned a good-natured, "Ew!" which made Owen giggle. At six and a half months old, he thought everything was funny.

As we all filed down the aisle, Abbie murmured in my ear, "I've gotta go change his diaper."

"Now?" I asked, gesturing to the important moment going on.

"I know, I know, but he went *as* Mom walked down the aisle. I can't just let him sit in it."

Connor made a face. "That's enough describing, okay, Abbie?"

"I'll be back as soon as possible," she said and headed across the sanctuary toward the bathrooms.

"How's she doing?" Connor asked.

"Better. She's gone back to totally freaking out when things go wrong. I never thought I'd be grateful for that, but I really am. I think she's done punishing herself for Owen. She's decided it's okay to be upset when"—I glanced at Chris, who stood oblivious across the room—"things don't go her way."

Connor rested his hand on the nape of my neck, squeezing in a way that made me tingle. "You're a good sister."

"I wasn't always."

"You are now." He pulled me close and kissed me. "That's what matters."

I watched Mom and Dad smiling at each other as if their years of miserable marriage hadn't happened. As if there'd been no affair, no packed suitcases, no squabbles about taking out the trash or who said they'd pay the electric bill but didn't.

Sometime when I hadn't been paying attention, they'd achieved that balance, the one I'd strived for since July 14. To not let my past take over my life, but to let it slowly and surely refine me into something new, something beautiful.

Something reinvented.

Acknowledgments

I've been overwhelmed with encouragement and support since learning the Reinvention of Skylar Hoyt series would be published. Many thanks to:

My husband, Ben, who told me I absolutely had to read *The Great Divorce* by C. S. Lewis, a tool that fleshed out Heather's background and her feelings. Thank you for your patience while I struggled to find the balance of the whole mom/writer thing. Couldn't have done this without you and your belief in me.

My daughter, McKenna. Thanks for not caring at all what I do for a living. You keep me grounded.

My parents, Steve and Beth Hines. There isn't room enough to list all the ways you've helped with the creation of this series, but here are a few highlights: encouraging my writing obsession from the beginning, free babysitting, randomly bringing over dinners, and promoting the books practically as much as I do.

My in-laws, Ann and Bruce Morrill. Thank you for adopting me into your family long before we shared a last name. And thank you for loving on my little girl while I work.

My one and only brother, Chris. Thanks for hanging around at book signings and being totally worthy of having a character named after you.

Bus, Janna, Leia, and Kylee Tarbox. Your enthusiasm for Skylar Hoyt caught me totally off guard. I'm so fortunate to call you guys family.

Roseanna White. Thank you for two and a half years of rejoicing when I rejoice and mourning when I mourn. And for regularly dispensing your grammar wisdom. God went above and beyond when he answered my prayers for a writing friend.

Debbie McCool, who's my real-life Heather. I'm so thankful for your wisdom and your belief in me.

Kelli Stouder, for your awesome gift of discernment.

Dr. Amy Knapitsch, who's stopped saying, "Uh, what's this for?" when I ask weird medical questions.

Elfie Rosario, my Hawaii expert. Thank you for not only sharing the books with your students but also educating me on Hawaiian customs.

The fabulous girls at Notre Dame de Sion high school here in Kansas City. Your support has been amazing and gives me energy.

My home church, Southwoods, and my "extended church family" at LifeStream. I'm grateful for how you embraced this series and supported me in my journey.

And the whole team at Revell. Thank you for all your hard work and for making me feel comfortable asking my newbie questions. Special thanks to Jennifer Leep for taking a chance on me, and Jessica Miles for your keen editing eye.

Stephanie Morrill is a twentysomething living in Overland Park, Kansas, with her high school sweetheart-turned-husband and their young daughter. She loves writing for teenagers because her high school years greatly impacted her adult life. That, and it's an excuse to keep playing her music really, really loud.

Don't miss the first two books

Getting a fresh start is harder than it looks.

Aster Flynn Wants a Life of Her Own . . .

But will her family get in her way?

New from bestselling author
Kristin Billerbeck

Daisy Crispin has a foolproof plan
to get a date for the prom.

Girls know all about keeping secrets,
but Sophie's is a really big one.

anything
but
normal

A NOVEL

Melody Carlson

Visit Melody Carlson at www.melodycarlson.com.